Contents

A LOVER'S *Heist 2*

ROME & LIRA'S LOVE STORY

K.L. HALL

A Lover's Heist II: Rome & Lira's Love Story
(Heist of Hearts Series Book 2)

K.L. Hall

Synopsis

Young and as picturesque as they come, Lira Armstrong is a college drop-out with a hustler's mentality. As a byproduct of the streets with two druggie parents, achieving her dreams of becoming a professional dancer hasn't come easy. When things with her boyfriend, Jevan, take a turn for the worst, she comes face-to-face with the man they robbed. Never in her wildest dreams did she expect him to be so heart-stoppingly handsome, let alone allow her to pay for her crimes in a different currency, sex. But when the stick turns pink, she finds herself embroiled in a pregnancy scandal that upends the foundation of her life.

Roman "Rome" Snow knows a hustler when he sees one, no matter how naïve Lira pretends to be. After all, she took part in his robbery, and *nobody* plays with his money. There's only one problem, he desires her more than any other woman, even the one he already has at home. After deciding to spare her life, he comes to her with an agreement to give them both what they want. She will be his for the night, and when the morning comes, she can leave. After giving in to his desires, the passionate gangsta soon finds himself torn between the one who feeds his wild side and the one who feeds his soul.

Newly married, Draya Snow has it all. Wealth, status, and a marriage where ménages and hall passes are a thing. Yet, her robust sexual appetite always leaves her craving more. When the news of Lira's pregnancy hits her ears, Draya finds herself on an unorthodox route to motherhood. Will she be able to control her festering jealousy to keep her marriage intact, or will she let her darkest desires come to light? This spicy novel shows the intricate dance of pillow talk and alliances, dominance, and submission and is for mature audiences only.

*Please note: This is the second standalone novel in the Heist of Hearts series. Each book in the series will feature a different member of the Snow family with no cliffhangers. *

Disclaimer

What you are about to read is for mature audiences only.
This novel contains:
Explicit language.
Adult themes.
Violence.
This shit is not suitable for readers under 18.
Reader discretion is advised.

*"And if loving you had a price,
I would pay my life for you"*

-Beyoncé—Part II (On the Run)

ROME

"What about that one?" I asked Draya, my eyes cascading over her right shoulder to the chocolate-colored girl rocking a pair of six-inch stilettos and box braids that brushed against her juicy ass.

"Which one?"

"The one with the braids," I told her before spilling some D'usse down my throat.

She slowly rolled her neck to peek over her shoulder. One glimpse, and she instantly rolled her hickory brown eyes at me while crinkling up her button nose.

"Are you serious? Look at those six-month-old braids, baby. Sis looks like she is about to loc up any second now. Anyone comfortable enough to go out in public looking like that doesn't keep up the maintenance downtown, and I don't want no parts," she declared, throwing up her hands.

Laughter drifted from my throat. Draya had a type, and she wasn't it. "I swear you're the pickiest person I know."

"Me? You're the pickiest of them all, Rome. Don't play with me."

"Only the finest pussy can ride this dick," I reminded her.

She smirked before wrapping her long nails around her martini glass and taking a sip. "And ain't none of 'em finer than mine," she boasted.

"It's your turn to pick, though, baby. Take a good look around. What do you want tonight? A redbone? A Latina? Or a taste of some sweet chocolate?"

"I'll know when I see her."

I nodded and let her scan her surroundings while perched beside me at the packed bar in downtown Atlanta. We'd spent the weekend there. I'd arranged a meeting with my connect for earlier that day. It had been almost nine months since we'd met in person. I'd been laying low and letting Baby take over my day-to-day shit while I made sure all my legal mess went away quietly. Luckily, my lawyers could get any evidence the Feds were trying to use against me thrown out because their informant, Giovanni, turned out to be unreliable after the shit he pulled with my niece, Dream. I wanted to kill him for what he did and all he tried to take from my family. Jail wasn't good enough for niggas like him, and I knew Chief wouldn't be fully satisfied until he was no longer walking the earth. Shit was far from over.

My phone vibrated in my pocket, drawing me back to my present surroundings. I smiled after reading the text confirmation that my shipment was going to Miami. That meant I would be able to relax and make Draya the center of attention for the rest of our quick getaway. Dray and I had been together for three years, and she was just as adventurous as she was the first day I met her. She was as free as they came but was loyal to me and only me outside the bedroom. Dray had a slim waist and a perfectly round ass standing at five-foot-five. She was from the same hood as me and liked to fuck the same bitches I did. She was every nigga's dream. Over the years, we'd had threesomes, foursomes, and even orgies. Nothing was ever off the table when it came to her sexual liberation.

2

"I think I got one," she mumbled without even taking her eyes off her prey.

I followed her expressive brown eyes straight to a doe-eyed beauty standing in the middle of the crowded dance floor with Brazilian weave down her back and dripping in chocolate skin from head to toe.

"She's beautiful."

"She's mine," Draya bellowed before taking the final sip of her drink. "I'll see you in a bit."

Draya kissed my lips, leaving a sticky sheen of lip gloss against them. I licked it off before finishing my drink and ordering another. All I had to do was sit back and let Dray do her thing. She'd call me when she was ready for me. She always did.

DRAYA

I MADE MY WAY TO THE DANCE FLOOR AS THE DJ SWITCHED THE SONG to *Sad Girlz Luv Money* by Amaarae and Kali Uchis, and I immediately started swaying my hips to the sexy beat. I continued to snake my way through the crowd, making my way over to the only person outside of Rome I wanted to get next to.

"Oh shit! This is my song!" she called out while winding her hips.

I bit my lip, watching the hem of her dress rise each time she popped her ass. "Girl, yes! Mine too! Your dress is beautiful," I complimented her while lightly brushing my hand across her exposed shoulder. Her skin was as soft as honey butter, and I could only imagine what it would feel like to be engulfed in the folds of her chocolate flower.

She flashed a winning smile at me. "Aww, thank you! I really like yours too."

I smiled back, glancing down at the plunging neckline on the revealing, sparkly red dress I wore before I continued to dance. I locked eyes with Rome from across the room and beckoned for him to join us. As soon as I felt his presence behind me, I pressed my ass against the natural bulge in his pants. It turned me on to know he was giving big dick energy even when his shit wasn't on hard.

The bass vibrated the floor underneath us as I threw it back. Once I realized we had gained an audience of one, I threw it back even harder before locking eyes with her. She shot me a devilish grin before throwing her hands in the air and tossing her head back to the sky, continuing to sway to the beat. I reached out to grab her hips and started pulling her closer to us. She spun around and pressed her back against me. I slid out from between her and Rome and let her wind her enticing chocolate hips against him while I grinded my ass against his back. For the song's duration, he was sandwiched between the two sexiest women in the entire club.

"Thanks for the dance," I whispered in her ear.

"No, thank you. You two are very...*hot*," she expressed with a slight smirk.

My lips curved upward to a smile. "You know what? You should take a shot with me."

Her chandelier earrings shook back and forth. "What? A shot? Noooo! I don't do shots!"

"C'mon, girl! My husband is buying!" I said, grabbing her hand and leading her back over to the bar.

Rome looked at me with an all-knowing look, and I shot him a quick smirk. "Baby, this is my new friend...."

"Amirah," she called out, filling in my blank.

"Amirah! This is my new friend, Amirah, and you're buying us shots!"

"Oh?"

"Yup!"

"I can't let him buy me shots. I don't even know either of your names."

I chuckled, knowing no woman truly ever cared enough to ask the name of whoever was buying her a drink as long as the shit was free. "I'm Draya, and this is my husband...."

"Roman," he interjected. "What will you two ladies be having?" he questioned, giving Amirah his undivided attention.

She locked eyes with him and immediately blushed. It was clear she found him attractive. Hell, any woman in her right mind would've.

"Tequila?" I proposed.

"Oh my God! You're going to get me in trouble!" Amirah bellowed.

"Good trouble, right? There's nothing wrong with good trouble," I said, tossing my arm around her waist.

Rome ordered a round of dark tequila for the three of us, and we took them to the head.

"Ah! That shot ran right through me!" Amirah confessed before sinking her teeth into the lime in her left hand.

"Let's go to the bathroom!" I suggested, scooping Amirah's hand in mine.

Rome made sure to keep his distance but escorted us, nonetheless. I loved that he let me be me. Most niggas wouldn't be cool with his woman fuckin' other bitches, but we had an understanding that didn't need to be explained to anyone who wasn't in between our sheets.

"I know you find him attractive," I said, eyeing Amirah's reflection in the bathroom mirror when she stepped up to wash her hands.

A wrinkle bridged across her forehead. "What? Who?"

"My husband," I clarified.

The thin hairs on her skin rose. "Um. I—I was just being polite, y'know? He did buy me a drink."

"Relax, Amirah. It's okay. I can tell he likes you too," I said, inching closer.

Amirah turned so that her backside was pressed against the sink. "I think I'm confused…."

"Let me make it clear for you. We're looking for a third. And you are too beautiful not to want."

I watched her brown cheeks turn dark red. "Draya, I'm flattered, but I've never—"

My lips cut hers off with an innocent kiss. "Let's just see where the night goes."

Standing light on her feet, she giggled while feeling the liquor run to her head. "Let's see, huh?"

"Yeah," I said, running the back of my hand down the side of her face. "You're so fuckin' beautiful."

She blushed, finding it difficult to maintain eye contact with me. "Thank you...and for what it's worth, I meant what I said about you and your husband on the dance floor. That was *very* hot."

"Let's make it hotter," I suggested.

When she didn't immediately respond, I took that as my opportunity to turn up the heat. Balancing on four-inch heels, I bent down to lift the hem of her dress and kiss her pussy through her panties.

She let out a soft hum and relaxed a few of her muscles, signaling me to continue. A smile snaked across my face before I slid her panties to the side and kissed her purring panther

before slowly slicing my tongue between her plump lips.

"Oooh shit," she moaned.

Amirah drew in a sharp breath the second my thumb pressed against her throbbing clit. "Mmm. See, you're already dripping," I told her before sucking remnants of her juices off my fingertip. Rome was in for a treat. She was chocolate just how he liked it with a pussy sweeter than grape Kool-Aid.

She looked down at me with a devious smile that encouraged my fingertips to plunge into her warmth. I had her body shaking so hard, that she didn't notice Rome step in and lock the door behind him. Any partygoers with a full bladder would have to wait. When she opened her eyes, she peered over my shoulder at Rome. One look at him and her chocolate thighs spread like Nutella.

"She's in," I whispered over my shoulder to him.

He cinched his arms around my waist before gliding his hands down my bare thighs. "You have such good taste, baby."

7

"I already know this."

Rome spun her around, gazing at her reflection in the mirror and the heavenly expression across her face. One by one, he placed her hands against the glass. He slowly lifted her dress and slid her panties down to her ankles. He licked his fingertips and cupped her pussy from behind. The savory sounds of her moans caused me to dive between my thighs to strum my clit like a bass guitar.

I stared into Rome's deep-set cocoa brown eyes as he held his stiff dick in his hand. "Let daddy come play in that throat."

Rome sunk his hands into Amirah's plump ass before my lips fastened onto his. Amirah and I dropped to our knees to suck his dick together, lathering it with warm spit.

He tossed his head back against the bathroom stall door as I ran my hands up and down his rock-hard chest. "Mmm, shit."

Amirah and I took turns licking up and down the base of his dick and deep throating his length while the other sucked on the tip and massaged his balls until the entire bathroom was filled with nothing but slurping and gagging sounds.

"Fuckin' spit on it," he instructed.

"Mmm. You like that, baby? You like it when we spit all over your dick?" I asked, sucking on the tip of his thick, curved monster.

"Oh, hell yeah," his deep voice vibrated as he palmed the back of Amirah's head.

I reached over to pull Amirah's hair away from her face as she bobbed up and down on my husband's dick—I'd never seen a sight more beautiful. My hands raced over her pierced, erect nipples, and she pushed out a soft moan. I hooked my fingertips into her plunging neckline and pulled down her dress just enough to expose her breasts.

My tongue toyed with her nipples. "Goddamn, you're perfect," I whispered to her.

"I think I wanna taste you," she whispered against my mouth.

I stepped back and propped my leg up on the counter, spreading my legs for her to taste the sweetness that rested between my cinnamon-brown thighs. "Bon appétit, beautiful," I purred.

Rome stepped up behind me and kissed my neck while Amirah's

lips got acquainted with my throbbing clit. "Ohhhh shit," I hissed, glancing at her.

"Is it good, baby?" Rome growled in my ear.

"Mmhmm."

"You ain't talkin' loud enough for daddy. I said, is it good?" he repeated.

"Yes! It's so fuckin' good! She's gonna make me cum if she keeps goin'."

"Yeah? She got you wet, baby?" he asked.

I gripped the back of her head before driving my hips forward. "She's got me so fuckin' wet, baby," I moaned before he kissed me.

"Good, now come get this dick," he coached before plunging into my flood from behind.

"Mmm, shit! Yes! Just like that! Make this pussy cum, baby!"

With my cheek pressed against the vanity mirror, I looked back at him as he served up back shot after back shot until I creamed all over his dick. Amirah's lips dominated his as he fucked me.

"That's so fuckin' sexy, baby," I moaned, watching him caress and grab her ass as their tongues made love.

After fucking me to my climax, I reached into my purse to pull out a gold wrapper and slid the condom over his dick. Rome held Amirah suspended in the air before pressing her back against the bathroom stall door and sliding her down on top of him. Her lashes flipped full-open as he fed her his snake inch by inch.

"Ooooh shiiiiiiiiitttttt," she squealed, eyes rolling in the back of her head the moment the hook in his dick hit her G-spot. At that moment, I was thankful that the 808s were vibrating the walls and suppressing her screams.

"Keep pumpin' that big ass dick into her, baby. Mmm, yeah. Just like that," I purred while finger fucking myself to the live porn playing out in front of me.

"You like this shit, baby?" he asked before licking her throat and swirling his tongue around her mouth.

"Mmm, you look so good when you fuck, daddy. Tell him how good he fuckin' feels!" I ordered Amirah.

Heels dangling in the air, she nodded with a soft whimper, unable to form a complete sentence. We all knew she was having the time of her life.

"Tell him to fuck you until you cum all over his dick!"

"Yes! Yes! Fuck me! Fuck me until I—I—I c—cum!" Amirah screamed while running her long, coffin-shaped nails through his soft, wavy hair.

"Mmm, shit. I think she's about to cum, baby. I can feel that pussy lockin' up on my dick," Rome hissed.

I gazed at Amirah's beautiful set of perky breasts bouncing in circles as he thrust into her.

"Oh, my fuckin' fuck! Keep goin'. Keep it right there! Don't stop! Don't stop!" Amirah squeaked.

"Take it. Take it. Take it," I coached, feeling my climax nearing as well.

"I'm c—cumming!" she screamed, panting uncontrollably.

"Mmm, shit. You ready to drink some nut?" Rome asked, pulling out of her and sliding off the condom.

Amirah eagerly tipped her head forward and dropped down to her knees before Rome covered her lips with his seed. I pulled her mouth onto mine, kissing his sweet nectar off her glossy lips.

As soon as I'd gotten cleaned up and walked outside the bathroom, I saw Rome standing off to the side with his cell phone glued to his ear and straight rage across his face. I slowed down my stride, trying to read the situation before approaching him. We'd had such a sexy ass time; I couldn't imagine why he looked so upset.

"Everything okay, baby?" I asked, gently putting my hand on his.

He looked at me with violence in his cocoa-brown eyes. "That was Baby. We need to get back to Miami tonight. One of our spots got hit."

4:27 A.M.

"One, two, three hundred thousand...." I said, stacking the money up in piles all around me on the thinly padded motel quilt.

I sat beside my boyfriend, Jevan, in nothing but a black cotton tank top and panties inside a seedy motel room half a mile away from the Miami airport. My eyes glazed over all the neatly stacked piles of money atop the bedding that looked like it had been in style in the sixties. I glanced over at him, and his tightened lips widened to a set smile.

"What are you smiling so big for?" I asked, already knowing the answer.

"I can't believe we pulled this shit off, Lira," he said, puffing from his blunt.

"Hey, you were the mastermind behind the plan, baby. I just drove the getaway car."

"Well, your driving got us almost half a million-tax-free fuckin' dollars!" he bragged before passing me the blunt.

I inhaled before smiling. "Yeah, I guess it did."

Stealing was nothing new to me. I'd been a hustler all my life. That's how I kept clothes on my back and food on the table long before Jevan even came along. I was the byproduct of not one but two crackhead parents, who both tried selling me for their next fix at one point or another during my adolescence. I never had anybody look out for me before Jevan and I met. Although we'd only been together for almost seven months, I loved him as much as someone who was never loved herself could. There were things he still didn't know about me, and there were things I probably didn't know about him, but when we were together, none of that shit mattered. I wasn't going to lie and say his actions didn't make me question his sanity at times. I'd watched him rob a stash house of one of the biggest dealers in the city, and he didn't seem to be the least concerned for his safety or mine. He was getting high and living in the moment. For the first time in my life, I finally had some real mothafuckin money.

"You sure you good?" he asked, eyeing me closely.

"Yeah, my—my heart is still racing."

He cheesed. "Mine too."

"I've never done anything this crazy before. I feel a rush inside me. We're so close, I can taste it!" I squealed.

"I can't wait to be as far away from this shitty ass city as we can be and start our new life together in L.A. The sunny breeze and palm trees of the West Coast are calling my name, baby!"

"And we will be tomorrow morning. I already booked the flights."

"I still don't see why we couldn't have left tonight. I don't know…I got a bad feeling about all of this," I admitted, unable to shake the rush of emotions flowing through me. I'd gone from relieved and excited, only for an eerie feeling to settle in the pit of my stomach. Smoking had only made me more paranoid.

"Stop stressin'. We gon' be good. I promise."

I nodded slowly before hitting the blunt again. "Okay."

"You trust me, don't you?"

My eyes landed on his warm, dark brown orbs, and suddenly all the butterflies tormenting my insides faded away. I bobbed my head and said, "Yeah."

"Look, Lira. You're the Bonnie to my Clyde. When I tell you I got you, I got you. I'd never lie to you about that."

I stared into his eyes before glancing upward at the small tattoo of an ace centered between his eyebrows. Jevan was a twenty-six-year-old hustler, who grew up in the Landover Projects and made his way through the streets. All I had to do was stay down long enough, and we'd been able to come up together. I glanced over at my suitcase next to his by the door. I couldn't wait until the sun came up in a couple of hours. I was finally going to be able to live a life that didn't consist of always trying to figure out where my next meal was going to come from, or if I was going to get locked up over some petty shit. Most importantly, I'd finally be able to go back to school and get my dance degree.

"I trust you, Jevan, but I worry about you sometimes," I admitted.

"Me? What do you mean?"

"This plan of yours...robbing Rome. I don't know him like that, but I've heard shit, and I don't think a nigga like that will take the shit lightly once he realizes his shit is gone."

"Bae, will you relax? Nobody knows we were the ones that took his shit except for the two people in this room right now, and I sure as hell don't plan on tellin' anybody. Do you?"

"Hell no! I'm not sayin' shit!"

"Me either, so we gon' be good," he assured.

I cocked my head to the side as I watched him shove the black mask he'd worn earlier that night into the trash can. "You never did tell me why you ain't like his ass."

"Who? Rome? What makes you think I don't like that light-skinned mothafucka?"

"First of all, you're just as light-skinned as he is," I chuckled, "but we specifically hit one of *his* spots because you knew he'd be out of town. That seems real...calculated. That's all I'm sayin'."

"Does it really matter?"

"If it didn't, I wouldn't have asked," I assured.

Jevan started shoving money inside a black duffel bag while he talked. "My older sister, Jhene, got mixed up with him some years back…and um, you know, she let all his money and shit go to her head and cloud her judgment. I told her not to fuck with that nigga, but she ain't wanna listen to me."

"The heart wants what the heart wants, I guess," I uttered.

"Yeah, well, her heart got her fuckin' killed. A nigga like Rome don't go long without making enemies, and one night they caught his ass slippin' right outside the club. They shot his car up with my sister inside. She bled out inside that nigga's whip."

I lowered my head in silence. "Oh my God. I'm so sorry, baby."

"Yeah. That nigga survived without so much as a scratch on his bitch ass head. Those bullets were meant for that nigga, not my sister! Since then, I've spent every day of my life wishing he'd die."

"So why not…you know, kill him? Why'd you want to rob him?"

"Like I said, a nigga like Rome doesn't go too long without making enemies, so I knew he'd have his brothers and goons ready to go at any given moment after that hit. He'd see me coming and trying to retaliate before I could even cock my gun. Nah, I wanted to hit him where it hurts the most, his wallet."

I nodded. "I understand."

"Do you really?"

"Yeah, family over everything. I can respect that, baby."

"Good," he said, pulling his shoulder-length dreads back into a low ponytail. "I'm tellin' you, them niggas ain't seen nothin' yet. That shit we pulled tonight, that's only the tip of the iceberg. When my brother, Bankx, gets out of jail, Rome and all them Snow niggas are gon' get that work. Believe that."

"What's your brother got to do with this?" I asked, secretly praying we didn't have to split our cut three ways instead of two.

"Everything."

A gentle puff of a laugh escaped my lips. "You're being kinda vague, baby."

"Look, my brother was locked up when all that shit with Jhene went down. Rome be on that street shit, and so do Bankx. And on the streets, it's a life for a life, and it's time for that nigga to pay up for what he let happen to our sister. It's been a long time comin', and I've been itchin' to come up off this nigga, but Bankx wanted us to wait."

I shot him a questioning brow. "Why?"

"He's comin' home soon. In another year or so, and when he does, Miami better take cover."

"How long has he been locked up?" I inquired.

"Eleven years," he answered.

"Wow."

"Yeah. He's been waitin' for this."

"Are you going to tell him what we did?"

"I will when the time is right. I wanna focus on us getting to Cali first."

I pushed out a muted sigh of relief before resting my head against the rickety wooden headboard. "You know, this is the first time you've ever talked to me about your family, baby. I know I don't have shit to share about family, but you have siblings. That's dope, the bond you have with them."

"Like you said, family over everything. And you're my family now, Lira."

Jevan walked over to put the bag beside our suitcases when his phone vibrated against the dresser. He picked it up and looked at the screen, sent a quick text message, and then slid it inside his pocket.

I snapped my neck at him. "Who was that?"

"Nobody, chill."

"If it was nobody, then why you tellin' me to chill?" I asked, bunching my arms up against my chest.

Jevan sighed and shook his head. Instead of responding, he walked over and crawled on top of the bed beside me like everything was all good. It wasn't the first time I'd caught some lame-ass bitch in his phone, and I was tired of him thinking I would take that shit lightly, especially when we got to L.A.

"So, you don't hear me talkin' to you?" I asked, cocking my head to the side.

He whipped his neck around to look me dead in my eyes. "Are you done?" he asked, gaslighting me.

"Hell no, I'm not done! What kind bitch do you take me for, Jevan? I'm not to be fucked with!"

"All I'm saying is we just hit one of the biggest come-ups, and you wanna argue about some bitch texting my phone? Grow up, Lira."

I rolled over on top of him, pointed my fingers in the shape of a gun, and slid them inside his mouth. "Look, this is the last fucking time I'm gonna have this conversation with you, nigga. Let me catch a bitch texting you at four in the morning again, and it's over for you *and her*!"

I snatched them away when he attempted to bite me. "You know I love it when you talk that gutta shit, right?" he admitted before snapping at my fingertips.

"Stop, Jevan! I'm not playing with your ass! I'm tired of you having me lookin' crazy out here to these hoes that you still feel the need to entertain! We've been together for seven months now. You've said it yourself you've never felt the way you feel about me before. I drove a getaway car for you! We're about to move across the country together. What more do I have to do to prove to you that I'm the only one you need?"

I felt myself getting emotional and tried to roll to the other side of the bed before a tear slipped down my cheek. If there was one thing I hated, it was looking weak, especially to a man. As Summer Walker would put it, I was simply *over it.*

He cleared his throat, deepening his voice before he spoke. "Lira, come here."

"No. Forget I said anything."

Jevan rolled over and pressed his dick against my ass. "I said come here," he whispered against the nape of my neck. *Fuck*, I groaned inside my head. His deep-throated voice instantly sent chills up my spine. Some seedy motel room was the last place I wanted to buss it open, but as long as I knew there was a higher thread count in my future, I didn't mind the celebratory fuck. In my mind, we'd finally made it.

"Jevan, stop."

He ran his hand down his thin mustache and goatee. "Oh, you really want me to stop?"

"Yeah, I do. Because you don't take me seriously."

"Nah, I don't think that's true at all," he said as he kissed my neck and nibbled on my earlobe.

"Ugh," I groaned. "Stop it. I'm serious."

"Not until you stop being mad at me," he said, licking his juicy, pink lips.

"I'm not mad, now stop!"

"Say it again, and this time, make sure you mean it," he said before stealing a kiss.

I pushed out another soft groan laced with aggravation. "I swear, I fuckin' hate you sometimes!"

"Yeah, aight. I love you too, baby girl, and I'm about to show you how much."

"Wait, you—you what? You love me?"

"You heard me."

"Say it again."

"You heard me say it already, Lira. Why I gotta say it again?"

"Because you've never said it before, and I wanna hear you say it all the time!" I squealed.

He looked me in my eyes. "Well, in that case, I love you. I love you. I love you."

"How much?" I asked.

"I'll show you better than I can tell you."

"Mmm. How you gon' show me?" I asked, sinking my pearly whites into my bottom lip.

He smirked, revealing the dimple in his left cheek. "By fuckin' that pussy on top of all this money!"

Jevan jumped up and shook out all the money from the duffel bag all over the bed. Benjamins and Jacksons were raining down on us like a money shower. "Oh my God, bae! Your ass is crazy as hell!" I giggled.

His crazy antics and that four-letter word instantly made my anger melt away. Jevan climbed on top of me and let his tongue gently part my lips. He kissed my neck as his fingertips slowly ran circles around my nipples, making them poke through the thin fabric of my tank top.

"Mmm," I moaned, knowing he'd hit one of my most sensitive spots.

I shivered in pleasure as his long tongue swirled across my chest, leaving a trail of kisses from my breasts down to the piercing in my navel.

"Mmm, shit, baby!" I cooed.

My body jolted forward when his lips clung to my sweet spot through my moistened panties. I shifted my body upwards as he slid them to the side and slipped his index finger inside me.

"Mm, this mine, right?" he growled.

"Yes, baby," I purred.

I looked in between my thighs and saw the passion flickering in his eyes as his lips gaped open, smacking against my moist, tender flesh. "Oh shit, don't stop, baby," I moaned while running my fingers through his dreads.

Jevan's lips glistened as he reached up to squeeze my nipples. He knew exactly what he was doing to me, each flick of his tongue and squeeze of my nipple inched me closer and closer to my peak. I was seconds away from cumming when the motel room door burst open, knocking our suitcases over in its wake. I screamed as Jevan quickly turned around. As soon as our eyes focused on who'd kicked in the door, we were both facing down Rome's gold-plated pistol barrel.

He clenched his chiseled, latte brown jaw before tightening his index finger around the trigger. "Move, and both you mothafuckas die."

My heart leaped out of my chest when Jevan hopped off me. "Fuck! Look, Rome—just chill out for a second!"

"Show me and my money some respect and put your fuckin' dick away, mothafucka," he growled.

Jevan slowly moved away from me and lifted his hands before submerging his stiff dick into his shorts. I clawed at the itchy quilt, pulling it over me long enough to put my titties away and inch to the edge of the bed to retrieve my jeans.

"Cornball ass nigga, you ain't gettin' no money, so you had to take mine, huh? Why'd you go and make the stupid mistake of fuckin' with me now? It's been years!"

"Beef don't die, nigga! Fuck you for what you took from my family!"

"This shit about Jhene, nigga? You know what happened with her was an accident! I put that on my life! I never meant for anything to happen to her. I paid my respects to your mother and your brother. I paid for her funeral and headstone because your fuckin' brother got caught up in the game and left all of you niggas with pennies! I took care of all of you when y'all couldn't because I fuckin' loved your sister."

"Fuck you and your money! The best is yet to come. You can believe that!"

"Yeah, aight, mothafucka. You'll never be smarter than me, lil' nigga. Remember that shit. Plus, you talk too fuckin' much about your plans! When are you gon' learn every nigga ain't *your* nigga?"

My eyes shifted from left to right, watching Jevan and Rome go back and forth until Rome got the better of him. In an instance, Jevan proved himself to be all bark to no bite, rushing to wave his imaginary white flag.

"Aight, aight. Look, this shit is between you and me. Just let my girl go, aight? She ain't have nothin' to do with it, I swear to God," Jevan pleaded.

Rome cast his cold, walnut brown eyes to me. "If he's tellin' the truth, then why the fuck are you sittin' here about to fuck on top of my money?"

"I—I," I stammered.

His squinted, icy glare didn't let up. "Is he tellin' the truth? You didn't have anything to do with this shit?"

I glanced at Jevan and then back at Rome, who was impatiently waiting for an answer. Still unable to string words together, Jevan spoke up on my behalf. "I brought her here. She ain't know nothin' about where I got it from, aight?"

"That's your final answer?" he asked.

"He-he's right. I—I didn't know nothin'," I confessed, hoping he couldn't see that I was lying through my teeth.

"So, you ain't know this was my mothafuckin' money all over the floor and this cheap ass bed?" he inquired.

I shook my head. "N—no. He ain't tell me nothin'."

"I find that funny. You wanna know why?"

I exhaled a trembling breath. "W—why?"

"I'd be a fool to not have cameras all around my shit. In places you'd least expect. All I had to do was run the tapes. I saw everything, down to the license plate on the piece of shit you mothafuckas drove away in. You think this dumb ass nigga is worth your life? Because that's what fuckin' with me costs you."

"I—I..."

"Shit, that nigga got you in here ready to fuck on my money. If anybody should be getting fucked on my money, it's me," he raged. "Now, get your ass up and pick up every last dollar of *my shit* and fuckin' hand it to me."

I scrambled to my feet and started picking up the money and putting it back inside the black duffel bag to hand it to him. I locked eyes with the skeleton finger bones tatted on his hands. Not once had his finger let up on the trigger. "H—here you go."

His eyes peered through me. It was as if I was standing in front of him wearing nothing but my cocoa brown birthday suit.

"That's a good girl. Now since it looks like I gotta teach both of y'all a lesson, I'll allow you to do one thing for me, and then I'll let you go."

"W—what?" I stammered.

"Shoot this nigga for disrespecting the game and stealing from me," he demanded before flipping his gun toward me to take.

My eyes swelled with fear. "Wait. What?" I asked as tears skydived from my quivering cheeks.

"Do it, or I'll blow both your heads smooth off," he warned.

Jevan had clearly thrown in a white flag, but Rome seemed to want beef still, and a bullet was forever. I was suddenly pinned between a rock and a hard place. All my life had been about preservation so much that my middle name may as well have been survival. But killing Jevan? The only man I'd ever allowed myself to fall for. I couldn't stomach the thought.

"Please—you've got your money. Can you please go?" I pleaded.

Instead of responding, he twisted his mouth into a frown. He swallowed my hand in his, placing my trembling finger on the trigger. "It's either you or him."

"Please...please don't make me do this," I begged, barely above a whisper.

"Yo, c'mon, Rome! Don't make her do this, nigga!" Jevan begged.

"P—please!" I screamed. "I—I can't do this! Please don't make me fuckin' do this shit!"

"Fuck it, your ass is takin' too long," he said before snatching the gun and putting two bullets in Jevan's chest that sent his body flying back against the nightstand. Speckles of crimson painted the peeling wallpaper and dust-filled lampshade behind him as his body thudded to the floor, his legs too weak to support him. I shrieked and darted to his side, reddening my hands with his blood as I held the sides of his face. His eyes had already begun to roll to the back of his head. He laid there, coughing as deep red, volcanic-like spurts of blood shot past his lips.

My hands quaked with fear. I'd never seen anyone about to take their last breath before. "J—Jevan, baby, it—it's going to be okay. You're going to be okay," I assured him, although we both knew it was the furthest thing from the truth.

Jevan tore his eyes away from mine, long enough to cast his fading gaze over my shoulder to Rome. "F—fuck y—you, nig—nigga," he expressed before going lifeless.

My eyes shot over to Rome's, eager to look at anything other than Jevan's dead body lying in my stick-like arms. Surprisingly, Rome's eyes were already trained on me. Desire seemed to radiate from his rigid, muscular body and intense eyes. It was chilling yet somewhat enticing. The eerie silence draped over us as I prepared myself to be the next to take my last breath. Before I could even process my next move, I felt his hand grip my wrist.

"Grab your shit. You're coming with me."

ROME

"WHEN YOUR WRIST LIKE THIS, YOU DON'T CHECK THE FORECAST. EVERY DAY it's gon' rain."

Lil' Baby's voice blasted through my speakers as I zoomed down the interstate with the mysterious chocolate beauty strapped in my passenger seat. I shot a quick text to Baby, Cash, and Chief, letting them know I needed them. I was already being watched, and I couldn't risk staying at the scene any longer than I needed to, especially with a witness. I glanced over at her, stealing a more prolonged gaze than intended. Her posture was hunched over, and her entire right side was glued to the passenger door to put as much distance between the two of us as possible. She sat with her eyes glued to her ring finger, chipping away the white polish on her fingernail. She was a sight for sore eyes from her beautiful oversized, plump lips and button nose to her long lashes fluttering up toward her perfectly arched eyebrows. Speaking of eyes, her dark brown orbs were low and troubled and told more of a story than I assumed her tightened mouth would ever allow. She wore her wavy, raven black hair pulled back into a low ponytail that dipped down to her lower back. As beautiful as she was, she'd seen and heard too much. I didn't know if she was the type to be bought or the type to run her mouth. Either way, I had to keep her in my presence long enough to find out what she knew and let her know how far I'd go to keep my secrets.

Chief was the first to hit my line. I answered and disconnected the Bluetooth so she wouldn't hear too much of our conversation.

"Yeah," I replied.

"Where are you?"

"En route to the crib. I got a package to drop off."

He exhaled into the receiver. "What the fuck happened?"

"I can meet you in thirty," I responded.

"Bet. I'll have Baby and Cash with me."

When we arrived back home, I turned to her as I killed the engine. The moment I reached over to her, she threw her hands up in defense, ready to fend me off if it came down to it.

"Yo, chill," I demanded, grabbing her swinging arm and crashing her back against my passenger seat. She jerked her neck in my direction, ready to bite my head off or burst into tears. Her facial expressions were all over the place.

"Wait here," I called out before tilting her trembling chin up toward my face.

I delicately thumbed away a speck of her boyfriend's crimson blood on her chin, saying nothing as I examined every bit of her beautiful, coffee brown face once more. I'd never been entranced by a woman before, and I'd seen some attractive females in my life. There was something different about her. Simply looking at her made my dick jump in my pants, which made her dangerous. I didn't know the first thing about her, but there was something about her I had to have. I exited the car quickly, putting the child lock on, before heading inside the house to find Draya.

"Baby?" I called out.

Draya popped around the corner from the kitchen to meet me in the foyer. "Are you okay, baby?" she asked, wearing a look of concern on her face and next to nothing on her body. She threw her arms around me, attempting to press her warm body to mine.

I took a step back, looking down at the dried specks of blood on my shirt. "I'm good. It's handled," I told her.

She eyed me closely before exhaling a sigh of relief. "Good."

"I need you to go put some clothes on."

"Since when do you ever ask me to put clothes on, baby?" she quizzed.

"I got somethin' in the car I need you to take care of for me."

"What is it?" she asked sternly, mood switching from concern to pure suspicion.

"You trust me, don't you?" I asked.

Her chocolate brown eyes rolled skyward before she smacked her suckable bottom lip. "You know I do."

"Good, then go get dressed. When you come back down, go out to the car and get her cleaned up. I wanna know what she knows before I figure out what I'm going to do with her."

"Hold up, baby. Who the fuck do you have in the car?" Draya inquired.

"The bitch that was with the nigga that stole my money. He was talkin' some wild shit, and I had no choice but to put 'em down," I admitted.

Draya's eyes flashed open wide with fear. "Y—you had t—to kill someone, baby?"

I sighed, unwilling to hide the truth from her. "I did."

"And who is this girl? Did she see you do it?"

"Yeah, she did."

After a brief pause, she let out a swoosh of air. "What do you need me to do?"

"Get her inside and get her cleaned up. Give her whatever she wants to get her head straight, and then bring her to me when I get back."

"Get back? Where are you going now? And what do you want with her?"

"I wanna talk to her. The nigga that robbed me wasn't any

stranger, Dray. I used to break bread with his ass way back in the day. If she was fuckin' with him, I wanna know everything she knows," I replied, only answering one of her questions.

"And what if she tells you somethin' you don't wanna hear?" Draya quizzed.

"Then, I'll cross that bridge when I get to it. She could be the key to stopping it before it starts."

"Or she could be the cause of why it does," Draya advised before strolling up the stairs to our bedroom.

"Cash will be here if you need him. I'll be back," I spoke at her back.

"Yeah, whatever."

I pushed Draya's words in one ear and out the other. I didn't have time for her feelings. I had to meet up with my brothers to finish cleaning up the mess I made.

"Tell us everything," Chief stated the moment I pulled up at the dock.

Baby, Chief, and I lifted Jevan's bagged body into the boat and headed deep out to sea. Once out far enough, we tied bricks to his chest to ensure that when we dropped him off the side of the boat, his ass would sink to the bottom of the ocean. We sat out there in silence for a few minutes, listening to the many sounds of the ocean at night.

"Well?" Baby asked, eyeing me. "What the fuck happened?"

"He robbed one of our spots. I got the money back. And I don't know, when I saw it was Jevan's dumb ass, something in me snapped."

"Why the fuck would he wanna shake your tree after all these years?" Chief wondered.

"That's what the fuck I'm sayin'. He had his girl with him, though… I gotta find out what she knows."

Chief's lips leveled with a frown. "Hold up, someone saw you, nigga? Where the fuck is she?"

"And why the fuck we only droppin' one fuckin' body out here?" Baby added.

A breath shuttled out my nose. "Listen, killing Jevan was…it was an emotional reaction, and I'm not gon' do that shit twice. I can handle this."

Chief's full lips thinned. "How, nigga?"

"I don't know yet. I need a little time to think," I told them.

"A little time? You ran out of time the minute you didn't shoot her ass when you killed her man! Where is she, Rome?"

"She's safe. I got Draya handling her at the crib, and Cash is there too."

"You got that bitch at your house, nigga?" Baby quizzed.

"Shut the fuck up, aight? When I say I can handle it without having another body on me, believe me, aight?" I asserted.

When we got back to the dock, Baby was the first one off the boat. "I hope you know what you're doing," he mumbled.

"Yeah, for all our sakes. She's not an orphan you can take in. She saw you kill her boyfriend. Where the fuck do you think her loyalty lies?" Chief grumbled.

"I hear you; I do. But I can tell she's scared. She ain't about none of this street shit. I need to talk to her and find out what she knows. After that, I'll figure out my next move."

Baby locked eyes with me while handing me his gun. "You know what you need to do, right?"

I pushed his hand away. "I know how to take care of it if it comes down to that."

"Yeah, you better. If you fuck this up, she could take our entire family down," Chief warned.

LIRA

My heart skipped a nervous beat when I heard a fingernail tapping against the window. A sigh of relief pushed past my lips when I saw a woman standing on the other side of the door instead of Rome. She clicked the key fob in her hand, allowing the doors to unlock before she yanked it open.

"Come on," she gestured, long eyelashes fluttering with each blink.

I shot my eyes at her, instantly determining her threat level. She looked to be about my height. Her skin was cocoa brown, and she had the words 'Queen B' written all over her. It was late as hell, and I could still tell she had makeup on as if she had to be camera-ready all twenty-four hours of the day. I frowned, refusing to unglue my body from the seat.

She snapped her fingers. "Did you fuckin' hear what I said? Get out of the car. Let's go!"

I reluctantly edged my body out of the seat and let my feet hit the pavement. Just as I extended my leg to take a forward step, she spoke up again. "Strip. Clothes go in the bag," she dictated, handing me a black trash bag.

"W—what?"

"If you think you're stepping inside with those bloody fuckin' clothes on, you're mistaken. Clothes. In the bag. Now."

I eyed myself closely as I stripped down to my bra, panties, and socks only feet away from the front door. What was left of my dignity had vanished entirely. I trailed behind her, reluctantly following her inside the prominent home and down a corridor to a dimly lit bathroom. I marched across the cool marble floor, noticing the sizeable round vanity mirror that lit up when I walked by.

"Towels are under the sink. Clean sweats and a t-shirt are on top of the counter. Get cleaned up and get your head together. I'll be back for you in thirty minutes," she claimed before turning away from me.

"E—excuse me. C—can you tell me what I'm even doing here?"

She sighed. "He wants a word."

My voice was quiet and tense. "He's got his money back, and my man is dead. What else would he have to say to me?"

She fluttered her long eyelashes at me as if I was annoying her. "That's between you and him. Just be thankful."

"Thankful? Thankful for what?"

"That he ain't leave that fuckin' gorgeous body of yours next to your niggas," she pointed out before closing the door behind her.

I turned on the shower and submerged my naked body under the water when the temperature was right. An outpour of tears washed down my cheeks as I scrubbed Jevan's dried blood off my skin. I felt disgusting. I wanted to scream, fight, cry, and throw up all simultaneously. It was the first instance I'd had to myself to digest all I'd seen. Somebody I cared for was gone, and there was nothing I could do about it.

I couldn't believe I was back where I fuckin' started and alone. My life was an ocean of tragedy. We were so close to getting everything we wanted. So close, I could taste the newness of a fresh start. To have it all snatched away in the blink of an eye and lose Jevan had me unraveling like a spool of yarn. That money was the reset button my life needed. Without it, I was nothing but a struggling college dropout with dreams of being a professional dancer. The bullet from Rome's gun seemed to have permanently popped that bubble. I'd been silently praying I'd wake up from the nightmare any minute, but it seemed to stretch.

By the time I got out of the shower, my fingertips started to prune. Running off no sleep and all the crying had me both physically and emotionally exhausted. After drying off and sliding on the t-shirt the woman gave me, I looked at my reflection in the backlit mirror. I was a fucking train wreck. Unable to stop the tears from flowing, I swiped my eyes when I heard a tap on the door. I pulled the sweatpants drawstring tight to fit my trim waistline when the door opened.

"You ready?" she asked.

"Uh, yeah. Just give me like a minute," I said, dabbing my puffy, red eyes.

She made her aggravation known through an open mouth sigh while picking up a washcloth and running it under the sink. "You missed a spot."

She dabbed the soft cloth against the back of my arm. "Look, I don't know what happened tonight or what you saw, but any nigga that would have you in the line of fire like that don't really give a fuck about you."

"My man did love me!" I affirmed.

"Bullshit. That nigga ever left you hanging without a plan?"

"You think any of that matters to me right now? My man is dead! He took a bullet for me tonight!"

"You go ahead and think that all you want, but that bullet already had his name on it. That nigga got you caught up in his shit. It might hurt now, but trust, if it were you in that body bag right now and not him, he wouldn't be shedding a tear over you. He'd be thanking his lucky stars that he could run off with Rome's money."

I tried my best not to show how angry I was, but internally, I was on fire. Even if what she said was true, I wasn't trying to hear that shit. Jevan wasn't perfect, but he was the only thing I had in this world.

"Besides, with a body like that, you're too fuckin' beautiful to let a nigga treat you like shit. Now let's go."

Knowing the option to refuse was off the table, I slowly trekked behind her. I followed her to a room a few paces down the hall. "Where are we going?" I inquired.

"Stop talking and walk. I told you Rome wants a word."

"Who are you to him?"

"I'm his, and he's mine. That's all you need to know."

"What is he going to do to me?"

She put her hand on the doorknob and twisted her neck in my direction. "I don't know. But we both know what he's capable of. The last thing you want to do is cross him twice," she warned.

I walked inside the spacious room that was almost too dark to see anything. The sound of the door closing behind me caused me to jump. Billions of thoughts raced through my head. My life was still hanging in the balance, and I didn't know how much longer I had to live. Shit, at the rate things were going, I didn't even know if I even wanted to be alive. Keeping a positive mentality was as draining as keeping a negative one. There wasn't a light at the end of my tunnel without Jevan and some serious cash to turn my life around.

An invitingly large bed rested against the wall with an oversized headboard behind it. The cloud-like pillows made my eyes droop even lower than they already were. I pushed my bare feet across the snow-white carpet to the balcony doors. My fingertips grazed the French door handles before stepping outside. The moist, warm breeze blew past my cheeks, pushing my saturated coils past my shoulder. Miami weather was always the stickiest at daybreak. Standing in the peaceful, unblemished silence, I finally felt safe enough to close my eyes.

My peace was interrupted by the creaking sound of the bedroom door opening. I flinched at the sound, turning to see Rome stalking my way. He seemed to wear a permanent scowl every time he looked at me as if the sight of me made him sick or like I was nothing more than a liability to him. My chest tightened with each step he took. I pressed my spine against the balcony railing. Rome approached me with skeleton finger bones tatted on his hands, a .45 by his gut, and his wet, curly hair slicked back into a low ponytail. It was the first time I'd gotten a clear view of him without tears stinging my eyes.

He brought a cold breeze with him, which sent a trail of goosebumps up my arms. His six-foot frame towered over me, face looking like the devil himself. As much as I wanted to hate him, something about his presence made the hair on my arms stand on end and my yoni throb. I stood erect, unable to take my eyes off him and move like I'd been cemented to the cool pavement underneath me.

"W—what are you going to do to me?" I asked, unable to stop my voice from shaking.

"What do you think I should do with you?"

My breathing accelerated as my body temperature rose to dangerous levels. "I—I—I'm s—so—sorry a—about your m—mo—money, o—ok—okay? I didn't k—know the t—two of y—you had h—history," I stumbled, unable to take my eyes off the gun at his side. I could only think about the worst-case scenario, which was me ending up like Jevan.

"I can't understand you if you don't stop crying."

He followed my eyes down to his waist, removed it, and extended it to me. "Take my gun. I'm not going to hurt you."

Beads of sweat populated on my lip and forehead as I shot my eyes up at him long enough to give him a look that said *I call bullshit.*

"This is the second time I've handed you my gun tonight. If I thought you'd use it against me, I wouldn't be offering it. Please. Just take it."

I drew in a deep breath and clipped my lips tight while holding my breath before removing the weapon from his hands. I tossed it to the ground and kicked it away from us before tearing my eyes up to his again.

He held his chin high and drew his shoulders back. "Feel better now? Feel safe? Now tell me what you know about Jevan and his family."

"Not much," I pushed out with a pensive expression across my face.

"What does *not much* mean?"

"H—he told me he has a brother that's locked up and a sister that died."

"And that's all?"

"Yeah."

"Don't lie to me."

"I'm not lying to you," I replied, tightening my jaw.

"So, if you don't really know shit about the nigga you were with, what the fuck do you know about the nigga you tried to rob?"

My shifting, bloodshot eyes found their way back to his pools of honey. He looked at me with a craving in his savage eyes. They were cold and empty like he didn't fear a damn thing, and at the same time, I'd never seen a pair of brown orbs more passionate.

"What's your name?" he asked when I didn't give him an answer to his first question.

"Why does my name matter if you're going to kill me?"

"Who said I was going to kill you?"

"So, you aren't?"

"I didn't say that either."

My chest caved with an exhale. "My name is Lira."

"What do you know about me, Lira?" he inquired.

The way he kept questioning me about what I knew told me that not only was he paid and passionate, but his ass was paranoid too.

"I've heard shit," I responded.

"Like what?"

"Like you're not to be fucked with...."

"And yet you fucked with me anyway. You're either the boldest female I've ever met or the dumbest."

"If you're not going to kill me, then what are you going to do with me? Let me go?"

"If I let you walk out of here, you know I'll be watching you, right?"

As much as I wanted to tell him that he'd be a fool not to watch me, I shifted my bottom lip underneath my teeth. "If I have to look over my shoulder for the rest of my life, you might as well kill me now."

He shot me a chilling stare while lighting and puffing the blunt he'd pulled from behind his ear in silence. "Are you tired?"

I frowned, not expecting an ounce of compassion to fly off his tongue. "What?"

"You look tired."

I instinctively rubbed the circles under my eyes. "It's like six-thirty in the morning. Of course, I'm tired."

"I'll have someone bring you food and drop you off wherever you want to go after getting some rest," he said.

My eyebrows squeezed together. "I don't...I'm not hungry," I claimed, clearing my dry throat.

Me and my empty stomach both knew that statement was false, but I would've been a fool to eat anything he or anyone else gave me.

"Rest assured; you're worth more to me alive right now. Get some sleep."

I didn't immediately object with no money and no real options lined up for my next move. Rome's promise to keep eyes on me had me planning to lay low. I intended to hold out on what Jevan had really told me about his brother's pending release and threat against Rome and his family. I knew the tidbit of information he shared with me could be worth more down the road. Knowing Jevan's secret seemed to be the best card I had in the bullshit hand I was dealt. Jevan's death would only fuel Bankx's rage whenever he found out. If he was getting out when Jevan said he would, Rome would have some heat coming his way.

ROME

Jarrell "Bankx" Carter had been a thorn in my side for years. He was a well-known Miami hustler that first put Baby and me on to the game. On the business side, things between us were always solid. It wasn't until I started dating his younger sister, Jhene, that things between us changed. He became envious and started mixing his personal feelings with our money dealings, and shit went left. The day the feds rounded him up, the streets began buzzing as if I had something to do with it, but I didn't. My brothers, Cash, and I were running a heist of our own that day. We'd lifted twenty-four kilos of gold bars and sold them to an international dealer for a return of over 1.5 million dollars, split four ways. I never intended to be near or talk to the feds. I was prepared to have a man-to-man with him whenever he got out if nothing else to talk about Jhene. I would never apologize about Jevan's bitch ass. He could feel however he wanted to about that.

My thoughts transferred from Jevan to Lira, who wasn't innocent, but she was no gangsta either. She was in over her head, and she knew it, but that didn't mean she had to lose her life because of it. To avoid having another body on me, I planned to keep a strict detail on her to ensure she didn't go to the cops about what she saw. I didn't take her as a snitch, but I couldn't be too careful. Her ties to Jevan were too close for comfort, and I knew people did crazy shit when they grieved. I also didn't know if she was a pawn in a bigger game, but if Bankx was controlling her from behind bars, I needed to keep my eye on her. She was the one person who could unravel my entire life.

I made my way into the kitchen, where Cash was heating some leftover McDonald's in the microwave.

"Yo, you good?" he asked me as the microwave beeped.

"Yeah. I need you to drop the girl off at whatever address she gives you and then send it to me. Get her to the car discreetly. I don't wanna wake up Draya, and I don't want her askin' a lot of questions."

"Bet. Where she at?"

"The room down the hall. And don't forget to send the address. I gotta have eyes on her at all times."

"For how long?" Cash inquired.

I shrugged. "I don't know yet."

"Aight, bet. Let me grab my food, and I got you," he stated.

We turned our attention to Draya, who walked into the kitchen and froze when she saw us. "Hey, baby," I greeted her, "what are you still doing up?"

"I came down here to ask you the same thing. Am I interrupting something?"

"Nah. Cash was just leaving."

With his food in one hand, Cash dapped me up with the other. "I'll get up with you later."

Once it was the two of us, Draya turned to me. "What did you end up doing with the girl?"

"Don't worry about it. She's being taken care of," I assured her.

She folded her arms across her chest. "In what way, Rome?"

"Since when do you ever ask so many questions about my business? You don't trust me or somethin'?"

"You know I do. I only want to know what I'm dealing with here."

I sighed, stepping right into what I was trying to avoid. "I'm going to have Cash drop her off, and then I'm gonna keep a strict detail on her and make sure she doesn't go to cops about what she saw."

"And you think that's enough?"

"If it's not, then it's not. Whatever it is, you ain't gotta worry about it."

She pressed her lips together in a flat line. "Mmm."

"What does that mean?"

She glanced down at the black duffel bag sitting beside the island. "Well, from where I'm standing, it looks like you got your money back and came home with a prize, too."

I shook my head in protest. "It's not like that."

"Then, tell me what it's like, baby."

"Shit, I thought you might like her," I joked.

"Now is not the time for fuckin' jokes, Roman. I'm serious!"

"And what if I was serious, too? It's my turn to pick, right? And I want her."

Her eyebrows jutted in surprise. "What? We've never, ever eaten in the same place we shit. Why start now?"

She'd posed a good question, but it was one I couldn't give her the answer to. Lira was too beautiful to kill. She was feisty and chocolate like I liked. I knew Lira was someone I could see myself having fun with, if only for the night, and that's when my wheels started turning. Maybe I could figure out a way to give us both what we wanted.

DRAYA

AFTER GETTING MYSELF UP AND READY FOR WORK, I CAME DOWNSTAIRS to grab a quick cup of coffee before heading out.

"Good morning, beautiful," Rome greeted me from behind the refrigerator door.

I grabbed my coffee tumbler out of the cabinet. "Morning, bae. Where are you going this morning looking all good?"

"I'm going down to the court for Dream's testimony at that bitch ass nigga Giovanni's trial. What about you? What you got planned after work?"

"Oh, uh, nothing special. Might get a pedicure after I get off," I replied. "How's Dream doing with all of this?"

"As good as to be expected, I guess. I'll find out more this morning."

My chin descended in a nod. "Tell everyone I said hey."

Rome walked over to me and kissed my cheek. "Okay, I will. Have a good day."

I felt terrible about Dream, especially having seen her and Giovanni together at the mall that day. I hadn't told Rome or anyone else about running into them. There was no glaring indication that something was wrong outside of her skipping school, which I checked her for. I had no idea he was that much older and doing things to her. If anything, that proved I didn't have a motherly bone in my body.

I got to work and sat my purse on my desk when there was a knock on my door. I spun around to see my supervisor, Tom, standing in the doorframe.

"Good morning, Draya. You got a second?"

"Uh, sure, Tom. What's up?"

"I'd like to speak in my office if that's okay."

"Sure. Let me turn my computer on, and I'll be there in a minute."

"You should come now," he suggested.

My eyebrows lifted in suspicion. "Um, okay, sure. Here I come."

I stepped inside Tom's office to see him sitting behind his desk and Mary from human resources occupying one of two available chairs. "Come in and close the door."

"This seems serious," I stated.

"Why don't you have a seat," Mary told me.

"I'll stand."

"We need to talk to you about the appraisal you did on the fifty-two carat canary yellow heart-shaped diamond. Do you recall?"

My heart leaped out of my chest. "Uh, yeah. It was rare. Only seventeen in the entire world, I believe. I appraised it for almost four million dollars, right?"

"Yes."

"What's the problem?" I asked, knowing he was referring to what Rome and his brothers stole.

"The problem is, the previous buyer recently sold it, and the new buyer had it reappraised only to find out it was a fake. Everything traced back to us, and he's looking to sue us."

"What? H–how is that our fault? How do we know that the buyer didn't switch out the diamond with a dupe after being bought from our auction house? I mean, don't we have lawyers or insurance policies to protect us against situations like this?" I rambled, trying to keep my composure.

"Draya, we've been going over the mountain of paperwork and investigations with our lawyers and the insurance company for weeks, and–"

"For weeks? Why am I finding out about this now?"

"Because we were instructed to keep quiet about it until the investigation was complete, and I'm sorry, but we will have to let you go," Tom announced.

I cleared my throat. "Excuse me?"

"The investigation concluded that it was your poor judgment as a product appraiser that compromised the integrity of this auction house. This was an enormous loss for us, and we can't afford another mistake like this."

"So, that's it? You're firing me?" I cut him off.

"I'm sorry, but our hands are tied," Tom confirmed.

I scoffed. "Save your apologies, Tom. I'm leaving."

I stormed out of his office and wiped the fake tears from my eyes. Little did they know, I didn't need their money. Once back inside my car, I started the engine and sat there gob-smacked. A part of me knew the day might come, but after months and months of waiting and nothing happened, I started to forget about it. I was just thankful the police weren't waiting outside for me when I stepped outside Tom's office. I loved my husband and the life his line of work provided for me, but I wasn't about to do jailtime. As much as I wanted to call Rome, I knew he wouldn't pick up because he was in court, so I decided to head to the nail shop to get my pedicure as soon as they opened. My phone vibrated in my hand, jarring me out of the umpteenth replay of my firing and into the present. I glanced down at the caller I.D., and a smile swung free across my face. I pressed to accept, and *his* sexy voice instantly sent chills down my spine.

"You know what I was just thinkin' about?" he asked.

"What?" I asked, gnawing on my bottom lip.

"You. Me. Fuckin' you over the balcony at the Ritz."

"It's not even nine o'clock in the morning yet, and you are already on ten," I judged.

"Always. But anyway, I'm surprised you answered. Shouldn't you be at work?"

I pushed out a short breath. "About that…I just got fired."

"What? What the fuck happened?"

"Eh, I'd rather not talk about it, if that's okay."

"You sound upset."

"I'm more than that," I admitted.

"Want to blow off some steam?"

I sighed as my foot pressed against the brake to stop at the red light. "I can't."

"You can't, or you won't?" he asked.

"You know what I mean."

I was glad Rome was out of jail, and things between us seemed to be running as usual as possible, but I couldn't pretend like I hadn't crossed a line while he was away. A line I'd been crossing at least once a week for months on end. I'd always been the type to see a line drawn in the sand and want to cross right over it. Maybe it was because I was a free spirit. Perhaps it was the thrill of it all. Whatever the case, I couldn't turn back. And each time I was underneath him, I didn't want to.

"Look, I know you're bummed out right now, but you're resilient, and you're smart. You'll bounce back from this. You can start your own thing, maybe get into real estate like you wanted. You can do whatever you wanna do," he assured me.

I grinned at his confidence builder. "Thanks. I needed that."

"Will I see your beautiful ass soon?"

I sighed. "I don't know, maybe. I'll call you."

"Try to enjoy your day, beautiful."

"Bye, you."

I pulled into the nail salon parking lot and killed the engine. The universe had thrown me a curveball in the form of a six-foot-two,

253-pound man that wasn't Rome, and instead of dodging it, I caught it, rode it, and tossed it back in every position I could. And if my husband ever found out about it, he'd kill us both.

"How was court?" I asked Rome as soon as he walked through the front door.

He made his way over to me with a pained look across his face. "Frustrating as hell. It took everything to not take that nigga Giovanni out right there in the middle of the courtroom."

"Yeah, I bet."

"How was your day?" he asked.

"Ugh," I groaned, "not much better than yours."

"What happened?"

"I got fired today, baby. They fired me over that canary diamond shit," I announced.

Rome's jaw clenched. "Are you fuckin' serious?"

"Yeah."

"Tell me everything they said to you, baby."

I shook my head. "It doesn't matter. It's over."

"No, tell me what they said."

"Something about the person who bought it from us went to sell it, and the new buyer got it appraised and found out it was a fake. I got caught in the crossfire because I was the one who appraised the original one, so they let me go."

"Are they going to press charges?"

I swung my head in a no. "They didn't mention any of that, thank God."

He walked over and pulled me into a hug. "I'm sorry, bae. You know I got you, right?"

"Always."

I followed him over to the couch and let him pull me down beside him. He tossed my legs across his lap and pulled off my heels before rubbing my feet. I threw my head back in pleasure.

"Damn, that feels good."

"I got you on the foot rub every night, baby."

"Can I get that in writing?" I inquired with an uneven smile.

"You can get anything you want."

"Ugh. I don't know. A part of me is like fuck it, whatever. Another part of me is like, okay, so now what? Like what's next for me?"

"Do you feel like you wanna find another job right now? I'm behind you if you do, but I'm also cool if you wanna take this time to lay up and have my babies."

I frowned. "Babies? Nigga. No. We talked about this. I'm good on the kid talk right now."

"I know. I was playin' with you, bae. Chill out. Relax. Woosah. Do you need a massage? You want me to roll you one? What you need, baby? Daddy got you."

I crawled into his lap and kissed his cheek. "Let me go take a shower, and you can do whatever you want to me."

"We only have an hour."

"Why an hour?" I asked.

"It's Gianna's birthday, and Chief wants everyone to come out to her party tonight."

I scoffed. "Of all nights to have a birthday party."

"I know, but he already had everything planned before the court date was set. He said he's poppin' the question to Gianna tonight. I know you don't wanna miss that."

"That's sweet, but you should go without me, baby. I'm really not in a celebratory mood. I'll stay home, and you can tell me all about it when you come back."

"You gotta come, bae. I need my lady by my side. Let's have fun tonight. It'll take your mind off all the bullshit from today."

I smacked my teeth. "Fine. Okay. I'll go," I agreed while rolling my eyes.

ROME

I COULDN'T HELP BUT CHUCKLE TO MYSELF AT THE IRONY OF CHIEF'S proposal. His ass talked all that shit about marriage and never doing it again, only to fall in love and bend that knee for Gianna as if he'd never felt that way. I was happy for him, though. Gianna was the person he needed in his corner, and I was glad they found each other.

"Congratulations, man," I said, finally making it through the line of well-wishers.

Chief pulled me into a hug. "Thanks, Rome."

"You a shit talker, but it's all love." I chuckled.

Laughter sprinkled the air between us. "Hey, when you know, you know."

I dapped him up. "Love is a beautiful thing, man. Enjoy it. Me and Dray gon' go head and get out of here. I'll link up with you soon."

"Aight, bet. Y'all be safe."

Draya and I walked out to the car in silence. She hadn't said much to me after Chief popped the question to Gianna. I couldn't tell where her head was at. My tongue burned with the urge to speak as I glanced over to watch her tapping her nails against her iPhone screen.

"We're good, right?" I asked when I stopped at a red light.

She tipped her head in a single nod. "Yeah, baby. We're golden. Why?"

"You've been on your phone all night, and I can tell you're sitting over there in your head, and I wanna know what's up."

She sucked her teeth. "My phone is nothin', baby. Shae's been textin' me all night with her man drama, that's all."

"Be honest. That shit still fuckin' with you, ain't it?"

She dispelled a lungful of grief. "I've never been *'quit'* before. I've always been the quitter. I've always been the one to leave before I get left, y'know? And I don't know, that shit took a bite out of my self-esteem, and it's fuckin' with me."

"What do you need from me?"

"I've got everything I need, baby. I'll get over it. I have to find something productive to do to occupy my time. I can't spend every day, all day, in the mall. People will start to think I work there." She snickered.

"Something will come along that'll pique your interest sooner or later."

"Well, until that day comes, you can have all my time."

Two and a half weeks later.

As the weeks went by, Draya seemed to become more distant. She was fidgety when she was around like she was always running late for something or had somewhere better to be. I knew Draya well enough to know when she was restless and in need of a release, but I still had my reservations about her actions. To take my mind off things, I

45

caught up with my brothers and Cash for a few pick-up games of basketball and drinks.

"Yo, how are things with the wifey? Everything good?" Cash asked me as we stepped out into the parking lot.

"Man, I don't know." I shrugged.

"What you mean you don't know?"

"I ain't wanna say nothin' in there, but she lost her job a couple of weeks ago, and ever since then, she's been acting fidgety and shit."

"Fidgety? What you mean?"

"Like she runnin' late for something important, but she's been askin' for rainchecks on our weekly lunch dates and staying out later with her girls and shit. I ain't no insecure ass nigga, but I also can't turn a blind eye to it when it's right in my face," I told him.

"You think she fuckin' somebody else?" he asked, glancing over at me.

"I know she likes to fuck bitches, but that ain't new."

"Nah, I mean another nigga, nigga."

I sucked my teeth. "Nah, man."

"You sure? You don't sound like you trust her too much right now."

"I don't know. Dray gon' be Dray, but she moving funny, even for her."

"What you want me to do?" he asked me as we approached my car.

I unlocked the doors while forcing out an exhale. "I want to put a detail on her. Only for a couple of weeks to see what she's up to. Nothin' drastic."

Concern pinched in the middle his forehead. "A detail? Do you think that's necessary?"

"I want it to be you, C."

He locked eyes with me as soon as he dipped his head inside the car. "What?"

"You're the last person she would suspect."

A quick no jerked his head. "Nigga, she knows my car. I'm the first person she would suspect!"

"Not if you do it right. You should be a fuckin' ghost. All I need you to do is follow her for a couple of weeks and let me know what she's doing. Be discreet about the shit, though, aight? I don't need her finding out about this. It's between you and me," I told him.

He bobbed his head. "Aight, bet."

I dropped Cash off back at his crib and headed to mine. On the way home, I got a calendar notification on my phone reminding me of my ex Jhene's birthday coming up in the next twenty-four hours. My abdomen pulsed with a hint of laughter, remembering the moment she plugged it into my phone and set an annual reminder for her birthday without an end date. It was the first time in years that the thought crossed my mind to delete it. Birthdays weren't my thing anyway. They hadn't been for some time. To most people, they were days to celebrate life, but for me, it was only an annual recap of the night that I couldn't delete, and a constant reminder of the moment I lost the love of my life.

The roads were slick with rain the night of my twenty-fourth birthday. I was dripping in ice from head to toe, sitting behind the heated steering wheel of my brand new polar white Mercedes. My windshield wipers whipped back and forth as I ran my hand up and down Jhene's exposed thigh. We were on our way to celebrate with my family and friends at the club.

"What do you think about the name Titan?" Jhene looked over at me and asked. "Titan Snow."

"Huh?" I asked, taking my eyes off the road to glance her way as a laugh emerged from my mouth. "That sounds like a Marvel character or somethin'."

"For a boy. Unless you want a junior."

"Doesn't every man?"

"What if it's a girl?"

I shrugged. "I don't know. Don't you think we should start telling people you're pregnant first before we start picking out baby names?" I asked, placing my hand on her flat stomach.

Jhene was only nine weeks pregnant but had been planning for the future since the moment the stick turned pink. She couldn't have been happier to become a mother, and I couldn't have been happier seeing her happy. As much as I wanted to show off my new ride, I would've been okay with curling up with Jhene in the crib.

"I told you we're gonna wait until I'm officially out of the first trimester."

"Why?"

"Because I don't wanna tell people, and then something bad happens."

"Why would you think something bad was going to happen? Ain't nothin' bad gon' happen to you, Jay. Not while I'm around," I assured her.

"I know, baby. Just let me have this one, okay? As soon as the first trimester is up, you can tell whoever and yell it from the rooftops if you want."

I pushed out a soft chuckle. "Bet. It's time to give Dream a lil' cousin anyway."

"Mmhm. A cute little girl cousin that looks just like her mommy," she joked.

I smirked. "I'm perfectly fine with that."

"This is a real nice ride," she expressed, complimenting my taste.

"Thank you."

"I'ma look real good driving it, too. Even better than you."

"I'm a tough act to follow," I assured her.

"You willing to bet that? Because pregnant or not, I'm pretty damn fly," she confirmed, flipping her long, skinny braids over her shoulder.

Jhene was strikingly beautiful even when she was being subtle. Her full lips were painted cherry red, matching my interior leather. She had a set of dramatic lashes fluttering over her bright cinnamon-brown eyes. Long, box braids cascaded down her back and framed her slender jawline perfectly. From the baby hairs swooped across her forehead to the Christian Louboutin heels on her feet, she was everything I ever wanted in a woman. She was the love of my life.

I spent the night trapped inside my head while Chief, Santi, Cash, and Baby's young ass lived it up in our private section. My eyes scanned the room back and forth as I toyed with the ring box in my left pocket. I'd been trying to find the perfect time to propose to Jhene all night, but it never seemed like the right time.

"Where's your head at tonight?" Jhene asked, tugging at my arm.

I exhaled before taking a quick sip of my drink. "I'm good."

"You keep lookin' like that, and I'ma make you take me home. My feet are starting to hurt anyway."

"Sit down then. You've been glued to my arm all night."

"Is it a crime to love being around my man?"

"You don't hear me complaining."

She unleashed a short laugh. "You sure about that? Because that just sounded like a complaint."

"Never that. You can be stuck to me like glue all you want. You say the word, and we can be on our way home."

"As long as I get a foot rub out of the deal, you got it, birthday boy."

I turned to face her, pushing a couple of braids behind her ear. "There's something I wanna ask you later. You know, when we're alone."

"Why don't you wanna ask me here?" she quizzed before kissing my hand.

"Because it's loud as fuck in here, for one. And two, I want you all to myself. You and my seed," I purred in her ear.

She pressed her chest against mine. "Sounds good to me. Let's go. I'll drive."

"No, you won't, Jay. Not tonight."

She smacked her lips before rolling her eyes. "You lucky it's your birthday," she teased.

"Mmhm. Let's say our goodbyes and be out. These niggas gon' party all night."

After we exited the club, we stood outside waiting for the valet to bring my car around when Cash called me back inside to settle a dispute with one of our waitresses. I'd charged over a stack on my tab before I left, and she had the nerve to complain about a few unaccounted for dollars. Cash kept offering to pay whatever the remaining balance was so I wouldn't have to go back inside, but she insisted she needed to use the card on file.

"Come with me. I don't want you standing out here alone while I handle this dumb shit," I told her.

She let her hand slip out of mine and shook her head. "The valet will be here with the car any minute. I'm a big girl, baby. I'll wait for you in the car."

"I'll be right back."

"Go. I'll be fine," she insisted.

I doubled back inside to handle my issues with the waitress and moments later heard gunshots ring out so loud, I could hear them over the blaring speakers. With nothing but Jhene on my mind, I raced outside to see her gasping for air and choking on her own blood. She'd gotten in the driver's seat. Why the fuck was she in the driver's seat?

Speckles of her crimson blood were painted across the dash and windshield as I pulled her out of the car and held her in my arms. "J–Jay, baby. It's gonna be okay. You're gonna be okay!" I assured her while stroking her face. "Somebody get some help! Somebody get some fuckin' help!" My voice cracked as I screamed over her shaking body.

Blood leaked from her nose as a single tear slipped down her face. "It–it hurts, b–baby...."

"Shh. Don't waste your breath, baby. Help is on the way," I proclaimed, hearing the sirens whirring in the distance. "All you have to do is make it to the hospital. Everything will be fine. I got you, Jay. Ain't nothin' gon' happen to you when I got you," I promised her, holding on tightly to her hand.

Tears stung my eyes as I gently wiped the blood pooling in the corner of her mouth as she flashed her fearful eyes up at me and tried to push out words. "R–Rome, I love y–y–you."

I cradled her head in my arms, trying to keep her tethered to earth, to me. I watched the glimmer in her eyes slowly extinguish. "I love you, too, Jay. Don't leave me," I demanded, leaning in to kiss her face. "Not like this, baby. No. Please, I need you to stay awake. Promise me you'll hold on until we make it to the hospital, baby. Just hold on," I cried, sinking my teeth into my lips, which were salty from tears.

"O–okay."

I watched her eyelids become heavier and heavier as the seconds fleeted past us, each one feeling like the span of a decade. "Open your eyes, baby. Open your eyes and look at me, Jay! Please! The ambulance is almost here! Wake up, baby. Wake up for me! Stay with me, baby!" I commanded, shaking her limp frame.

I pressed my back against the bullet holes in my driver's side door, refusing to speak what my mind and heart already knew. Jhene was gone. I leaned in to kiss her lips for the last time, knowing life had left her body.

LIRA

Each week that passed, Rome made sure to make his presence known without even bothering to show his face. I left his home with my life and more trauma than I bargained for. He kept his word and had me followed. It didn't matter if I was at work, at the grocery store, or in the privacy of my apartment; there was always a black truck with dark tint parked outside, watching me. He wasn't trying to be subtle. He wanted to keep himself at the forefront of my mind, and he'd succeeded. For three nights in a row, he'd been the invasive species in my dreams. Each head trip hotter than the last.

I'd been stewing, laying low, and minding my business. I spent night after night on my feet at the waitressing job I had to beg to get back after things with Jevan fell through. Losing Jevan still weighed heavily on my heart, but I wasn't in the right mindset to grieve. I missed him. I hated him. I envied him. I'd be a liar if I said I didn't feel like he got off easy. Yeah, he lost his life, but he didn't have to spend the rest of his days above ground looking over his shoulder or waiting for the other shoe to drop. He was my ticket out and left me with nothing but a pocket full of sorries and a target on my back. I was a fool for thinking something good would come out of doing something so damn bad. All the red flags were presented from the start, yet I did it anyway, eyes wide open. I didn't plan to give Rome a reason to kill me, but it didn't mean he wouldn't find one.

After arriving home from a long night, I stalked up to my apartment building. My eyes zeroed in on the running black truck parked across the street like clockwork. It was always the same damn truck. I was tired. I was irritated, and suddenly, I couldn't take it anymore. Instead of heading inside as planned, I stormed up to the truck and banged my fist against the window.

"I fuckin' see you, okay?! Stop following me!" I swore before the driver inside the car sped off. Rattled, I hurried back across the street and into my apartment building. When I got to my floor, I saw a large dress box leaning against my door with a black satin bow tied around it.

A frown creased my face as I kicked it over to ensure nothing would jump out at me. When nothing eventful happened, I unlocked my door and carried the box inside. The bow slipped off and hit the floor as I uncovered the black tissue paper to see a snow-white one-shoulder dress with a high slit up the left side. Underneath it was a notecard that read, *"Dinner at 7 p.m. tomorrow. A car will be out front to pick you up at 6:30 p.m. Wear the dress. -RS"*

I scoffed. The fuckin' nerve of that nigga to leave only his initials as if he was *somebody.*

"I'm not goin' to that fuckin' dinner," I groused.

I paced back and forth across my living room, debating what to say. I take that back. I knew what to say, but I wanted to figure out how to say *'fuck you and the horse you rode in on'* tastefully.

"Who the fuck does he think he is? Requesting me! No, demanding my presence!" I griped. "I'm not! I'm not going! Nope. Not goin'. Nah. No way. No. Hell no!"

For twenty minutes straight, I paced and cursed back and forth. Trying to talk myself out of it only tossed gasoline on my fiery rage. The only, and I mean the only reason I could even think about obliging him was to tell him to go fuck himself in person, bullet be damned.

The next night, the dress somehow managed to find its way from the box to my body, and it felt damn good on my curves.

"I'm glad you could join me," Rome greeted me when I arrived at his front door.

The scent of his pheromones alone had me in a trance. I could see how a woman could easily lose all self-control around him. Rome was a whole problem and nothing to be fucked with, but I still wanted beef.

"The invitation you left at my front door didn't seem optional," I quipped.

"You're right; it wasn't."

"Why am I here? Because I know it's not for dinner."

Lust rested in his eyes as I sauntered past him like everything around me was in my name and not his.

"Then, why did you come?"

"The only reason I came was to tell you to your face to stop fuckin' following me! I already told you I ain't no snitch, and I think I've proven that."

"I told you what would happen if I let you leave, didn't I?" he asked, tongue tracing his bottom lip.

My lips pushed out a maddening sigh as he watched my every gesture. I felt his energy vibrating even with eight feet between us. My eyes soaked him in. He was clad in a white, short-sleeve polo shirt with a crisp, folded collar. It was unbuttoned at the neck, exposing his neck and collarbone tattoos. I noticed how everything he was wearing clung to him like it was painted on. From the way, the fabric hugged his chest, down to the jogger sweatpants around his waist that hugged his muscular calves and left nothing to the imagination about what laid alongside his left thigh.

"If the following doesn't stop, maybe I should go to the police about what I saw!" I spat, tossing out the only card I had to play.

"Is that a threat?"

"Is the following going to stop?" I replied with a question of my own.

He turned away from me. "Follow me."

I huffed, ready to let him know that stalking down the hallway and away from me didn't end our conversation. I followed him into the dining room with a table set for two. A frown creased my face.

"You think a simple dinner will rectify what you took from me? Jevan was important to me!"

"I don't see you shedding any more tears."

"Grief manifests differently on everyone," I retorted.

"You should never shed a tear over any nigga that would put you in that situation."

"You don't know shit about Jevan or me, so spare me the chat as if you give a fuck about my well-being."

"If I didn't, your body would be sinking to the bottom of the ocean next to your man. Now sit down, and I ain't askin'," he barked.

I took my seat and crossed my arms across my chest like a brat. As much as I wanted to bite back, I had a lump in my throat the size of a melon. Instead, I focused my eyes on the covered dinner plate in front of me.

"Open it," he suggested.

I cut my eyes at him before pulling the lid off. Instead of seeing a plated meal, there was a document on the plate. I frowned. "What is this?"

"An agreement."

"To what?"

"You allow me one night with you in my bed, and when the morning comes, you're free to go. That is, if you agree, you won't run and tell the cops what you saw."

"And if I do?"

"If you decide to break this agreement and go to the cops, we'll have to make other arrangements," he said vaguely.

I scoffed. "What else do I have to do to prove that I ain't no snitch that doesn't involve fuckin' you? My body ain't for sale," I confirmed.

"But your freedom is. You said it yourself; you want the tailing to stop, right?"

I shook my head as my eyes glazed over the three pages of legal jargon. He must've been out of his fuckin' mind. Bat shit crazy.

"I guess you're one of those niggas who likes to play with his food before eating it, huh?" I asked, rolling my eyes.

"Only when the food looks as good as you," he said, smoother than Rico Suave.

"Am I really that intriguing?" I inquired.

"What?"

"Answer me. Am I? Am I so desirable that you just have to have me, knowing that we both know what I know? You took something from me, yet you want me to give something to you. I don't see how I get anything out of the deal, so no, I think I'll pass on gettin' dicked down by the nigga that killed my fuckin' boyfriend!" I hissed, pushing myself away from the table.

He pulled the lid off his plate, revealing a gun. I froze as my heart galloped in my chest. "Rome–"

"I won't have a choice," he confessed.

I flashed my eyes up at his and saw the sincerity written across his face. I couldn't consider it. I wouldn't. Could I? Would it be so bad if it meant I got to walk away? Or was the bullet the better choice? I slowly edged myself back in my seat and gave the papers another once over.

"No strings?" I asked.

"None," he confirmed.

"One night?"

"One."

"And there's no more looking over my shoulder and shit? I walk free?"

His eyes worked me over. "You have my word as long as I have yours."

Fuck, I thought to myself. My mind ran a million different scenarios. If one night on my back meant that I could press the reset button on the rest of my life, I'd do that. On the other hand, he could fuck me and put a bullet in me right after. Then it would have all been for nothing anyway. I knew firsthand I couldn't rely on the police to protect me. Everybody was out for themselves, and I had to look out for myself. The only way out was the way through.

He handed me a pen. "Read over it and sign at the bottom of the last page saying I have your full consent. After our night, we go our separate ways, and you'll never see me again as long as you keep your mouth shut."

Heartbeat racing, I scanned the contract for the third time. It was filled with disclaimers, waivers, and enough lawyer talk to choke on. "How do I know you won't put a bullet in my head when it's over?"

He chuckled. "You'll be fine."

"I'm serious."

"I promise I'll take good care of you."

My heart skipped a beat. Signing meant asking for trouble, but I'd be lying if I said a tiny part of me wasn't at least a little bit intrigued at the entire thing. Rome was easy on the eyes, in shape, and had a head full of gorgeous dark hair, amongst other desirable features. It was human nature to find him attractive. Allure aside, was I willing to spend one night dancing with the devil? After all, he *was* an angel once upon a time.

One week later.

I signed my name on the dotted line, and before the ink even dried, my schedule was filled with appointments for STD/STI testing and bloodwork, a massage, manicure, pedicure, and waxing. After receiving a clean bill of health, I headed to my wax appointment to meet my waxer, Nia.

"Lira?"

I nodded as I stood to my feet. "Yes."

"Hey, I'm Nia. Nice to meet you. Follow me back."

I followed her back into a private room and started to undress.

"Have you ever gotten waxed before?" she asked.

"It's been a minute," I answered.

She grinned with elation. "I've been Draya's personal waxer for a couple of years now, so I assure you, you're in good hands."

"Draya is, um, she Rome's...." I asked, intentionally letting my sentence trail off, hoping that she would fill in the blank.

"Yeah. She's his wife."

My eyebrows heightened, and I froze with my pants around my ankles. "Wait, what? W–wife? She's his wife? They're married? Oh my God!"

"Girl, chill."

Air leaked from my throat as I immediately began to redress. "No! Hell no! I'm not doing this! I'm sorry I wasted your time, but I have to go."

She chuckled. "No, you really need to chill. Rome and Draya are not your average couple, trust me."

"What does that even mean?" I asked, frustration laced in my tone.

"I'm just saying, they send special clients to me, so I know all about what you're about to do, and you won't catch any judgment from me, okay?"

"So, this is a normal thing for him? To fuck other women, and she's okay with that?" I quizzed in disbelief.

"Mmm. How do I put this? Draya's a...free spirit. She, well–they partake in the freakier side of things."

"Freaky things like what?"

"I shouldn't even be tellin' you all this because it ain't none of my business, but let's just say, she likes eatin' pussy as much as he does."

I groaned. "What the fuck."

"Listen, whatever you decide to do when you leave here is your business, but they already paid me, so you may as well get a free wax while you're here."

With my head spinning in a million different directions at once, I huffed. *Why the fuck didn't he tell me he was married?* I wondered to myself as I undressed and laid across the table on my back. Nia stood off to the side and began churning the hot wax like butter. I twisted my neck in her direction and caught her flipping through a textbook while waiting for the wax to get to the perfect temperature.

Curious, I asked, "What are you studying for?"

"I'm in school to be a nurse. This waxing shit is cool and all, but it's temporary. A bitch want more, y'know?"

"Yeah, I get it. I was in school, too."

"Yeah? For what?"

"Dance."

"Dance? That's what's up. What do you wanna do with that?"

"Eh, I didn't finish. I had a semester's worth of classes left and lost my scholarship. You know, life," I explained.

She jerked her chin in agreement. "I feel you. It be like that sometimes. There have been plenty of times I've wanted to quit or do something else. School is stressful as hell."

"You can say that again."

After Nia waxed me from brow to booty, I tossed my clothes back on and grabbed my purse. "Thanks."

"You're welcome. Hey, listen. Um, Draya's cool, but don't cross her. Y'know?"

A quick exhale passed through my nose. "I have no intentions of doing that."

"Good. Because one thing about her, when she wants something, she usually gets it. Rome's a boss in his own right, but she's got him wrapped around her finger. You seem cool, so y'know, whatever you decide to do, remember what I said."

My freshly waxed eyebrows squeezed together. "Uh, yeah. Thanks for the advice."

I walked out and got back inside the backseat of the truck that Rome had sent to escort me to all of my appointments. The driver took me to Rome's house since the wax appointment was my last one. I spent the entire drive trying to figure out what I was going to say when I saw Rome. I didn't care how freaky he and his wife were; they were married, and I wasn't a homewrecker. When the car came to a halt, the driver came around and opened the door for me, but I refused to get out.

"I want to speak to Rome. I want to speak to your boss," I demanded. "Have him come out here and talk to me, or I'm not getting out of this truck!"

The driver stormed inside and, a few minutes later, came back with Rome trailing behind him. "What's wrong?" Rome asked, with a frown across his face.

I peered at him through the cracked window. "Why didn't you tell me you were married before I signed that stupid contract?"

He bit his lip. "Whether I'm married or not doesn't change anything."

"How can you say that? It changes everything! This shit was already crazy from the start, and now I have to find out that you're married right before I'm supposed to sleep with you? I can't."

"You know what will happen if you don't," he answered. A spark of chaos ignited in his eyes as they bore into mine. It was the same look he had the night he killed Jevan.

I pushed out a heavy sigh while staring down at my painted nails. "I'm not sure I can do whatever it is you want me to do when I get out of this car, Rome. Even if your wife is okay with whatever you do, what does that mean? Is she going to be in the room? Am I supposed to let her touch me too? I've never been with another woman before, much less a threesome! I mean, she's beautiful; I just–"

"Draya and I have more than an understanding about tonight. This isn't our first rodeo, and you don't need to be afraid. I want to make sure you're comfortable, so tell me what you want."

I flashed my eyes up at him. "What if I don't know what I want?"

Rome's gorgeous brown eyes looked at me with no judgment whatsoever. "If you want it only to be me and you tonight, then say that."

"We can do that? What about your wife?"

"Draya can do her own thing. Are you comfortable with her still being in the room?"

"I don't know. I guess that's fine," I agreed, knowing I would have to give in to something.

"Okay. Take a minute to get yourself together and come inside when you're ready," he declared.

"I'll come in a minute," I confirmed, heart racing to dangerous levels.

The first thing my drifting eyes landed on when I stepped inside his bedroom was the pack of gold wrappers on his bedside. He was standing off to the side, pouring himself a drink and then two more.

"Here," he said, extending a glass to me.

Draya looked at me, only wearing a matching lace bra and panty set, and flashed a perfect rank of teeth in my direction before passing him the blunt she'd just hit. "Don't worry, I don't bite," she assured me.

I glanced at her with a pensive look across my face before tossing the liquor Rome had given me down my throat in one big gulp.

"You smoke?" Rome asked, offering me his blunt.

I reached out for it. I was ready to feel nothing and everything simultaneously and prayed I didn't remember most of it when the morning came. After a couple of puffs, I passed it back to Draya. I tossed down three more shots before the buzz of the weed and liquor overcame me. Finally feeling light on my feet, my muscles relaxed.

Rome looked me in my hazy eyes as he swiped some curls behind my ear. He pulled my body close before gently pressing his lips against mine. I slowly parted my lips, allowing his tongue to enter my mouth as he entangled his fingers in my hair. My nipples hardened underneath my dress as his thumbs moved in a circular motion against them. Lips still intact, we inched backward until I felt the edge of the bed against the back of my legs. I eased to a sitting position, slowly lowering my body onto the bed. I uncrossed my legs, silently inviting him to touch what was in between. Instead, he climbed in between, hovering over me as his hands started to peel my dress away from my body.

His hands skittered down my chest. "You're so fuckin' beautiful."

"She looks good enough to eat," Draya added, admiring every inch of me from afar.

Their carnivorous eyes devoured me as if I had the golden Willy Wonka ticket between my thighs. The lower Rome's hands went, the more I trembled in excitement. I suddenly didn't want him to go away.

I slowly ran my tongue across my lips. "Thanks."

His warms hands found my waist and then traveled to the hem of my dress. The fabric slid up my thighs, stopping right underneath my ass. Rome's orbs tore across my smooth, bare skin.

"Relax for me," he said before sliding his tongue inside my open mouth.

I closed my eyes and let my body sink into the soft, lavender detergent-scented sheets underneath me. Soon, my dress, bra, and peek-a-boo panties were puddled at my feet. I laid underneath Rome, clad in my birthday suit, as his chest pressed against mine. I clawed at his shirt while his fingertips found the entrance to my warmth. He pushed his most extended finger inside me while eyeing my pussy.

"Mmm, she's beautiful," he grunted out.

A soft moan escaped my lips. "Mmm."

He placed my hand on the bulge in his pants, and I gulped before slowly massaging his erection. Each second that passed, the more I became a slave to my body's impulses. I wanted him more and more.

"You want it? You gotta make that pussy cum for me," he directed, twisting and turning two fingers inside me. "Show me how wet you can get."

I looked over his shoulder and caught a glimpse of Draya. Rome looked down at me, almost as if he could read my mind without me saying a word. He turned to face Draya.

"She wants to know if I have your permission, baby."

Draya walked up to the side of the bed and rested her hand on Rome's broad shoulders. "Yes. I wanna watch you destroy that pretty fuckin' pussy, baby," Draya announced before flicking her tongue against his earlobe.

Elated to entertain herself, Draya walked over to an upholstered chair in the bedroom corner and started to put on her one-woman show. While she massaged her clit and fingered herself, Rome began to mark his territory across my body with his tongue. He made a trail of kisses from my neck down my chest, stopping to suckle on both nipples.

"Mmm. Shit. You look so damn good right now, baby," Draya called out.

Rome continued to dip his fingers in and out of my sweet spot before adding his tongue. I instantly drove my hips forward, feigning for more.

"Oooh shit," I groaned.

"Tell me what you want me to do, baby. Get me right, Daddy," Draya whimpered.

Rome pushed my legs up, aiming them toward the heavens. "You know I wanna see you fuck with that pussy for Daddy," he told her.

"I'ma fuck with this pussy for you, baby. Mmm, shit. I'ma cum if I keep goin' this deep."

"Go deeper for Daddy, Dray," he coached her while his lips were slathered with my juices.

The way he suckled my clit had me ready to shed real tears. He continued to coach his wife through her nut while feasting on my yoni. My toes were too busy throwing up gang signs at the ceiling to focus on anything else but that. Hearing her moans and erotic commentary in the background made him work harder, which made me even wetter.

"Ooooh shit, baby! I–I'm cumming!" Draya squealed.

"Mmm. Make that pussy cum one more time for, Daddy," he instructed.

My back arched as I palmed the back of his head. "Don't s–stop. Don't stop. I–I'm about to c–cum," I whimpered.

A harmonious combination of our screams and moans filled the room as Rome tongue-fucked me to ecstasy. He pulled his shirt over his head and completely undressed. "That first one was on the house. I'ma make sure you earn your next nut," he said before flipping me on my stomach.

Rome hiked my ass up in the air before feeding his dick to me from behind.

"Ahhh, shiiiitttt!" I screamed in pleasure.

"Mmm, shit. Every time I hit that spot, I want you to tell me how good it fuckin' feels. Every. Fuckin'. Time," he demanded, delivering deep stroke after deep stroke.

"So good. It makes me feel so good," I moaned.

He spanked me. "You want me to stop?"

I bounced my bubble butt against him, feigning to feel every inch. "No! I never want this to stop!"

The dick was better than good. It was breathtaking. Majestic. State-of-the-art. Unrivaled. No man had ever been able to do to my body what he did or reach the depths he'd achieved.

"Listen to that shit, Dray. You hear how juicy she is?" Rome asked, glancing over at her.

I cast my eyes over in her direction, watching her hands slip and slide back and forth across her clit. She didn't look to have a care in the world as she watched her man fuck the shit out of another woman right in front of her. She seemed to enjoy it. Draya deserved a medal of honor for willingly sharing it. I wasn't that gracious.

Switching positions, Rome flipped onto his back and pulled me on top of him. I inched down his rod, burying him deep inside me. He caressed my shoulders and ran his hands across my neck before his tongue slithered straight up my throat.

"Mmmm," I moaned, bucking against him.

His fingertips spread rambunctiously through my tousled curls, gently massaging my scalp before he twisted a handful and yanked my neck back.

"Ride this dick like it's yours," his lips mumbled against my quivering chest as his tongue danced across my nipples.

"Ooh fuck! This feels so fuckin' good," I purred, eyes rolling backward.

"Mmm, this dick got your kitty weeping," Rome whispered against my sensitive flesh.

"You like how she ridin' that dick, baby?" Draya questioned.

I tossed my hair to the side to look back at her. She'd managed to make her way from the corner of the room to the foot of the bed and was tugging on her hard nipples.

"Yeah, I do," Rome answered her.

"Fuck yeah. Give her that dick, baby. And you better ride that shit," Draya said, directing her attention to me.

I glanced over at her once more, noticing her lust-drowned eyes were already locked on me. "Ride it just like that. Yeah, that's a good girl. You look so good riding his dick," she purred while spreading her legs across the bed.

My teeth clung to my bottom lip as I watched her in a trance. There was something about her seductive chocolate eyes that were almost hypnotizing. She slid her hands up and down her perfectly sculpted body that oozed sex from her head to her pink-painted toes. "Mmm, Rome. She looks like she's about to cum."

I looked down at him, grinding harder. I pushed my hands into his chest and popped my ass on him. I'd give them one if they wanted a show, especially if it meant edging myself closer to another mind-shattering orgasm.

Rome gripped one ass cheek while smacking the other. "Ride that shit, Lira. It's all yours. Ride it like it's all yours," he coached.

"Fuck! Give it to me! Fuck! Oh my God!" I screamed. I was on the brink of my umpteenth orgasm, and it felt just as wet and wild as the first. "I–I'm a–about to c-cum!"

"Cum on every inch of this fuckin' dick, Lira," he commanded before hooking his tongue around my nipple.

"Ooooh shiiiiiiiittttttt!" I screamed, feeling the familiar rapturous wave wash over me once again.

Rome's hands remained glued to my hips as he drove them backward and forward against him. He slowed down the pace, thrusting in slow upward motions to allow me a few seconds to recover before switching positions and fucking me some more.

LIRA

There was something to be said about the morning after my night with Rome. He'd certainly left his mark on me, yet no omelets or cheese eggs were being made when I woke up the following day. I got my shit, and I was gone. In truth, it was good he sent me on my way when he did. I didn't know how many more orgasms my pussy could take. I'd cum before, but *never, ever* like that. Rome's wood was as long as a phone number, *area code included.* I'd be lying if I said all ten inches didn't have me walkin' sideways when I left or if fragments of the night we shared didn't invade my dreams from time to time. I didn't understand how something so real could feel so dreamlike.

After the heat of the moment faded, I spent every waking moment after that looking over my shoulder. I noticed every car that seemed to linger outside my apartment a little too long or the black sedan parked outside my shithole waitressing job every night after closing. There wasn't a doubt in my mind that Rome was still having me followed. Yet, it was the present moment I was in that felt like a nightmare. Bad things always seemed to come out of nowhere and without warning.

"Hold the absorbent color change tip in your urine stream, or in a sample of your urine collected in a clean, dry container, for just five seconds," I muttered out the directions for the home pregnancy test in my left hand.

There had to be another reason I was late. I was only taking the test to clarify what I already knew to be true. I wasn't pregnant. I'd been stressed to the max without Jevan and without anything more than the dead-end waitressing job I started with. The same dead-end waitressing job I had to beg to get back. After peeing on the stick, I picked up my phone to set the three-minute timer. When the alarm dinged, I swiped the stick off the edge of my bathroom sink, fully expecting to see the words *not pregnant* staring back at me. Instead, only one of those words was on the screen.

My heart rate quickened. "Pregnant?" I whispered. "What the fuck?"

We spend our entire lives worrying and dreaming, planning for the future, ordering our steps to how we're going to achieve these goals we set out for ourselves, but no matter how much we plan, we're never prepared for unforeseen changes—the inevitable curveballs. My fingertips fumbled over the box as I pulled out the second test. I flung the stick in the trashcan with haste and stormed out of the bathroom to get a water bottle so I could pee again. I chugged half the bottle of ice-cold water while looking around my apartment and what limited furniture I did have. I sold as much as I could and put whatever was left in storage, thinking Jevan and I would start fresh in California. When that shit fell through, I opted to use the open space as my dance studio and sacrifice the luxury of coming home to a nice couch and other shit that made a house a home. In my living room, all that was left was a beanbag chair in the corner, two large wall mirrors, and a TV stand with a decade-old flat screen. I was grateful I hadn't officially skated out on my lease and had something to fall back on. It wasn't like I ever had many guests over anyway. Dancing was the only thing that kept me sane. I was so determined to get my dance degree that I'd saved up my tips to go back to school. I needed at least twenty thousand dollars even to be taken seriously at the financial aid office since I'd lost my scholarship.

The second test showed the same result. I fell across my bed and buried my head in my hands. Life was hard enough; I didn't need to make it worse by bringing a baby into the world. Besides, I'd never even toyed with the idea of becoming a mother, especially not when the father was the man who killed my boyfriend.

DRAYA

I WAS ENJOYING MY *ME-TIME* AT MY PRIVATE SHOPPING APPOINTMENT AT the Gucci store. I'd spent the last couple of hours lost in the Design District. When my cell rang, I was trying on something from their vintage collection in the dressing room. My teeth peeked through my lips when I glanced down at the caller I.D.

"Hello?" I answered.

"I thought you were supposed to be shopping," the person on the other line said.

I smirked before stepping out in front of the mirror to look at the satin dress from all angles. "I am. I'm in the dressing room trying on a dress, if you must know."

"Mmm. That shit looks good, too."

I twisted my neck in the direction of his extra-soothing voice. My eyes crinkled with a smile. "What are you doing here?"

"Your nigga got me watching you, remember?" Cash's grin skewed.

I stepped up to him, encircling my arms around his neck. "You're my little secret. You good?"

"You know a nigga cooler than a cooler, especially now that I get you all to myself."

After my mid-day rendezvous with Cash, I headed to the other side of the city to run a few errands before heading home. I parked my car on the side of the street and hopped out when I saw Lira coming out of the building where my gynecologist's office was. Initially, I hadn't planned to speak, but when I saw her, my mind was flooded with flashbacks of the night she'd spent in our bed.

"Lira?" I called out.

She stopped dead in her tracks. "H—hey…"

"How have you been?"

"Good," she sputtered out, eyes pinging from one direction to the next.

I watched her shift her weight back and forth from her back leg to her front. It was clear she was uncomfortable in my presence, so I decided it was best to keep our interaction brief. Before cracking open my lips to say goodbye, my curious eyes fell to the ultrasound sticking halfway out of her bag. I snatched it out. "What the fuck is this?"

"Draya, listen. I never meant for any of this to happen!"

"Any of what to happen?" I asked, looking down at the long reel of fetus snapshots. "Are you pregnant?"

"Yes. I was trying to wrap my head around it all, but you don't have to worry. I don't plan on keeping it."

"Worry? Why would I worry?"

"It's Rome's baby…" she confessed.

I couldn't believe my ears. "What the fuck did you just say?"

"The doctor confirmed I'm seven weeks pregnant, Draya…."

Later that night, Rome sat across the dinner table with concern plastered across his face. My ears were still burning from the bomb Lira dropped on me. I was sick to my stomach all the way home, debating whether even to tell Rome or act like I never found out. I didn't have a motherly bone in my body, but I wasn't down with some other bitch carrying my husband's seed. We'd had dozens of bitches in our bed and never once had a pregnancy scare. My wheels continued to turn, churning out one conspiracy theory after the next. Maybe the hoe came here and saw what life could be like and was lying. Or maybe she was really carrying her dead nigga's baby and was trying to pin it on Rome to get paid. Or perhaps I didn't have anything to worry about at all. Whoever's baby it is, she said she was getting rid of it. Even with that settling feeling, my curiosity still ate away at me.

"You okay, babe?" Rome asked, snapping me out of my thoughts.

"Me? You're the one with the weird look on your face. Are you good?"

"Yeah. You have been a little off since you got back home today."

"I'm, uh…actually; I do have something to ask you."

"What?"

"Did something happen with the condom with Lira?"

A wrinkle cut across his forehead. "What? No. Why?"

I let out a sharp exhale. "I ran into her today coming out of the gynecologist's office."

"Okay, and?"

"That bitch is pregnant, Rome. She's saying it's your baby."

ROME

I sat at the dinner table with my head spinning while Draya got up to put her plate in the sink as if she hadn't dropped a nuclear bomb on me. After the momentary shock paralysis wore off, I followed her into the kitchen.

"What the fuck did you say?" I asked.

Leaning over the sink, Draya snapped her neck in my direction. "You heard exactly what I said, Rome. She's pregnant."

"And how does that make the baby mine?"

"You tell me! You were supposed to use a fucking condom! You always use a fucking condom!" she screamed in my face.

"I did!"

"Then,., what the fuck went wrong?"

"I–I don't know, okay. Let me just talk to her and figure out what's going on. There's got to be an explanation for this shit."

"What is there to talk to her about? She said she's getting an abortion, so it really doesn't matter who the father is. End of discussion."

"What?" I questioned.

"That's what she told me she was going to do."

My lips twitched downward. "Then, why the fuck would you even tell me she was pregnant in the fuckin' first place?" I roared.

"Because if we're going to keep doin' our thing how we like to do it, we gotta keep it tight, baby! No more fuckin' slip-ups, okay?"

My mind raced back to that night. I remembered pulling the roll of Magnums off the nightstand and sliding one on. I remembered how fuckin' creamy she was. I remembered how good it felt being in between her chocolate thighs. I remembered the enticing sound of her moans. I remembered looking at her as if she was the only woman in the world. Other than that, the night was one fragmented blur after the other.

I let out an exasperated sigh. "Aight, aight. You're right. No more slip-ups," I agreed.

Draya ejected an tight-lipped huff before draping her arms around my neck. "Good. All we have to do is follow up and make sure that bitch does what she's supposed to do and get rid of it so all of this can go away."

I peered down at her. "You know having kids was something I always wanted, though, right?"

"Of course, I do, but we're still practically newlyweds, Rome. And having kids was something we agreed we'd talk about later down the road."

"And here we are at the end of the road, Dray. She's pregnant, and I think it's time we take it off the backburner and talk about this if the baby is mine," I said sternly.

She let her arms fall to her petite waist and took a step back. "So, you want the bitch to keep it?"

"If it's mine, I do," I expressed without a second thought.

Draya's face turned stone cold as a tear slipped down her eye. "Do you even love me?"

"You know I do. Why would you ask me some shit like that?"

"If you did, you wouldn't be doing this to me, Rome. I'm your wife! Why would you want anyone to have your child but me?"

I reached out to grab her shoulders. "This isn't how I wanted any of this to happen, Dray, but if she's telling the truth, then this is something we have to deal with as adults."

"Aborting it is dealing with it as adults! Suddenly, you wanna be a father so bad that you'd be willing to let a bitch that stole from you have your fuckin' baby?" she questioned.

"She'd just be having it. I'd want the two of us to raise it."

Her brows squinched together. "W–what?"

"Nothing changes between you and me. If she's telling the truth, she's not going to be my baby mother, Dray. She'll be our surrogate, and you and I will raise my child together."

Her hands flew up in the air before she shook her head. "Rome, I don't know the first thing about kids. I'm not ready to be someone's mother!"

"This is going to bring us closer together, Dray. I can feel it," I assured her.

"In what way? If anything, it's pushing us apart! I feel like you're booting me into the passenger seat, and what I say in this relationship doesn't even matter! You're rushing this. Admit it!"

"Everything is always your way, Dray. All the time! I give you everything you want without question. Always have. You wanna eat some pussy? I'll let you call over whoever. You wanna take it a step further and do some swinger shit; then I follow your lead. But the one time out of all the many times I've ever fucked another bitch, she turns up pregnant, and you wanna abort it without even giving it a second thought? I can't stand by that. Not until I know if it's mine."

Fire glittered in her eyes. "So, I'm selfish because I don't want some random one-night fuck to carry my husband's baby? Well then, so fuckin' be it, Rome!" she reeled.

"Draya, I'm not sayin'—"

"No! What you're saying is clear. This new baby that we don't even know is yours is all of a sudden your number one priority! It's crazy, Rome! You sound fuckin' crazy!"

"Crazy because I'm not running away from my responsibility if it's mine?"

Her eyes bugged wide before she exploded. "You're taking on

fictional responsibility when you just said you don't even know if it's yours!"

"I'm gonna find out."

"How? Huh? By asking her nicely if you're her baby daddy? She helped a nigga steal from you, and you're rewarding her?"

"I got my money back."

She smacked her lips while shooting me a thorny look. "Are you saying you would've killed her instead of having her in our bed if you didn't? Because if that's the case, I wish you wouldn't have gotten back one red cent! Fuckin' think with your head and not your dick! How much can we really trust her?"

I spewed an aggravated huff from my nose. Arguing about it was getting us nowhere. We were no closer to the truth, and I could feel a headache coming on. "I'ma take a ride," I announced, deading the conversation where we stood.

"So, that's it? You're just gonna walk out? Niggas wanna talk about responsibility! What about your responsibility to me, Rome? Huh? I'm your fuckin' wife!" she cursed at my back.

I let the front door close behind me, praying the fresh air would do me good, and hopped into one of my rides. After merging onto the interstate, I navigated to the store to pick up a few different brands of pregnancy tests and headed over to Lira's place. Moments after I knocked, the door swung open, and I froze. Seeing her face again was like drinking water after spending a lifetime in the desert. She took one look at me and let a sigh pass through her twisted lips.

"So, I take it she told you?"

"Yeah, she did."

"Bet you wish you'd killed me now, huh?" she expressed with a cynical chuckle.

"No," I answered.

My eyes had been milking her in since she opened the door. Instantly, flashes of our night began to replay in my head. It had been weeks, but the brown beauty standing in front of me was someone I was secretly glad I had a reason to run into again.

She shot me a puzzled look. "So, you're not mad?"

I found myself staring at her kissable mouth. "No."

"What's in the bag?" she quizzed, drawing me out of my head and back into the moment.

I held it up before handing it to her. "Here."

She took it and looked inside. "Pregnancy tests? Why do I need these? I went to the doctor, Rome. I have an ultrasound with a fuckin' picture of a baby on it. It doesn't get any more real than that."

"Well, can I come in so we can talk about it?"

"What is there to talk about? The appointment is set," she blurted out.

"How far along are you?"

"Seven weeks."

"And you're sure you haven't had any other partners after me?"

She gathered her arms across her chest. "No." We stood in her doorway in silence before she spoke up again. "Look, I didn't mean for or want any of this to happen."

"What if I said I wanted you to keep it?"

My question brightened the whites of her eyes before her lips downturned. "Why would you want me to keep it? You don't even know me."

"I know I don't know you, but I want you to keep it."

I had two separate women, and neither wanted any parental responsibility. I laid down and made a child. That type of responsibility didn't just go away. I was willing to do whatever I could to ensure my seed made it into the world.

She belted out another cynical chuckle. "Oh really? And how does your wife feel about that? Because something is telling me you jumped out the window on that one!"

"It doesn't have to be all bad. Hear me out."

"What do you mean?"

"Look at it as a surrogate arrangement."

"Like I would have it, and then...."

"And then my wife and I would raise it. You're off the hook after nine months."

"Listen, I'm sure maybe something like this could work out in another parallel universe, but having a baby would be the icing on an already pretty shitty cake. I don't see you changing my mind about that."

"I'll pay you a quarter of a million dollars."

Her eyes diverted to me with a look across her face that said *are you serious?* "What?"

"You heard me."

"You're gonna pay me a quarter of a million dollars to carry this baby?"

"Yes."

"No strings?"

"There may be some."

"Like what? Name them."

I scanned the room, and blaring police sirens whirred down the street outside her window. I took note of the lack of furniture inside her empty apartment. "If you're having my baby, I want you to stay in my home. Not in my bed, but in my home so I can make sure you get the best possible care."

"What's wrong with me staying here? I know it isn't much, but it's mine. I don't have a problem taking care of myself and keeping track of my doctor's appointments, Rome. You don't have to breathe down my neck about it for the next few months."

"I'd feel more comfortable knowing you had access to everything you needed over the next few months until you give birth."

"Half a million," she negotiated.

A smirk slid up one half of my face. "Excuse me?"

"If I even have to consider living under your roof and being under your watchful eye for the next few months, I want half a million."

"Fine. If you agree, we'll need to make an appointment for you to get a paternity test done. Is that something you're willing to do?"

"I'm not lying about you being the father, Rome. We both know what happened to the last person I was with before you. This is your baby."

"If you want the money, we have to be sure."

"Okay, if it's safe, then fine. I'll do it," she agreed.

"Okay. Once that's done, I'll arrange for half the money to be given to you and the other half when the baby is born."

"And how do I know that you're not going to cut me out of my other half once the baby is born? I want the rest of the money the second I go into labor; that way, we both have what we want at the end."

"Fine."

"And you're sure Draya will be okay with all of this? Especially me moving in? I'm fine right where I am."

"She's my wife. She'll stand by whatever decision I make."

"And what if I don't know if I want to stand by your decision? After all, it is my body."

"I know that."

"Can I think about it?"

"How much time do you think you'll need to figure out if you want to become half a million dollars richer?" I bargained.

She tried her best to smuggle the dawning of a smile. "Shut up! It's bigger than that, and you know it. This is a life-changing decision."

"You're right. It is. Take all the time you need, but not too much time."

She twisted her lips. "Bye, Rome. I'll let you know when I know."

Six days later.

Weed smoke exited my nostrils as I sat and played a chess game against myself. My cell phone chimed, canceling out the peaceful silence I'd been sitting in. I flipped it over to see a text from Lira saying she would agree to keep the baby and be our surrogate pending one condition. Bitten by excitement and curiosity, I called her instead of responding to her message.

"Hello?" she answered.

"So, you made your decision?"

She let out a sigh. "Yup, pending one condition."

"And what's that?"

"If I agree to move into your house as your surrogate, you can't touch me *ever* again. This is strictly business."

My lips twisted. Her condition was something I hadn't thought about until it hit my ears. "Strictly business, huh?"

"Strictly business," she repeated.

"Okay then."

Later that day, I moved forward with having contracts and paperwork drawn up about our agreement, had the first-floor suite cleaned and prepared for Lira's pending arrival, and worked with my accountant to arrange an awaiting payment of half the agreed-upon amount. Once the paternity test was done, I'd have him send the money straight to her account. Draya was still uneasy about the entire thing. She'd never had a problem expressing that. Ever since I told her about Lira becoming our surrogate and the agreed-upon payment, she'd become even more distant.

"This won't work if you're not one hundred percent on board," I said as she passed me to go into the laundry room.

"You knew I was zero percent on board from the beginning, yet she's still going to move into our house," she retorted.

"It's temporary, Dray. It's all temporary. It's still you and me, but we can't look divided when she gets here. We have to put up a strong front. We look weak right now."

"Weak?"

I cut her off before she had a chance to react negatively. "I'm not calling you weak. I'm just saying that I'm sure it must feel like shit is on fire all around us, but it's not, baby. We gon' get through this together."

"How can you be so sure?"

"Because sometimes the best gifts come in small packages."

She scoffed. "More like surprising fucking packages."

I released a tight breath. "I know you're uncomfortable, bae. This is uncharted territory, but you've got to give me some effort. You have to. Tell me what would make you feel comfortable."

"I don't know. I just need some time and space away from all of this."

"Away from me?" I questioned.

She forced out an exhale then recovered her breath. "I'll let you know when I know."

I knew Dray like the back of my hand. Whenever she was feeling too tied down to something, she'd want to break free, no matter what. To her, our relationship had shifted to something more grounded out of the blue, and she needed the space to regroup and get comfortable in the uncomfortable.

"I'll book you a flight. Just let me know where you're going."

"I will."

LIRA

IN ALL, ROME'S TENDERNESS ABOUT THE ISSUE SURPRISED ME. HIS offering me half a million dollars to carry his baby threw me for an even bigger loop. Positivity wasn't something I'd expected from him, given our history. Yet, I'd agreed to carry the seed of such a passionate gangsta. We'd gotten the paternity results back, proving what I already knew, he was the father. Even after the first check was deposited into my account, I still didn't know how I felt about loaning my body to a baby for the pregnancy, but the money and the surrogacy loophole of not having to raise the baby after it came out was a comforting thought. I wasn't someone who had a good upbringing or superb role models, nor did I have a family legacy to pass down. I wasn't ready to become someone's mother.

A couple of days after the check cleared, I quit my waitressing job and drove straight to the University of South Florida financial aid office to officially re-enroll as a full-time student. I hadn't expected the pregnancy to be the silver lining I'd been waiting on, but Rome had unknowingly handed me my way back in. I still had to audition to get back into the program, but I made sure I was more than prepared.

For years, I'd put my body through rigorous training in hopes to one day have a professional dance career. I smiled a cramp into my cheek as my eyes cruised over the admissions pamphlet. There was a bullet stating that almost ninety percent of their graduates landed a job within six months of graduation.

"I emailed over all my paperwork. Did you receive it?" I asked, nervously sitting across from the financial aid advisor.

"Yes, I did," she said, clicking away at her keyboard.

I glanced around at the green and gold USF paraphernalia adorning her desk. "How much is it for me to re-enroll? And are there any additional scholarships I can apply for?"

"The check you sent for the amount listed in the email was sufficient."

"Really? So, does that mean that I'm–"

"Yes. Welcome back to the University of South Florida, Miss Armstrong. Proud to have you as a returning USF Bull!"

I cheesed, showing all thirty-two of my teeth. "Thank you. Thank you so much!"

I stepped outside the financial aid office and drew in a deep breath. USF was home, but something in the air felt new. Now that I was officially back in school, I headed over to the library to submit my audition video of myself in choreographed dance performance to start the process of fighting my way back into the competitive dance program. I'd taken all my prerequisites from the history of modern dance to improvisation and was ready to dedicate the next four and a half months to myself and achieving my goal. Once I was an official college graduate, I planned to start lining up dance auditions in Cali the moment I had the baby. I'd never been more motivated to line up everything so fast, but the baby in my womb may as well have been a ticking timebomb. I had to move as steadfast as possible before I started showing.

I ran my hands through my hair and expressed a celebratory smile as I clicked submit on my audition video. While I sat back and waited for my answer, I decided to focus on packing up what little belongings I did have before moving into Rome's house. Had the pregnancy not aligned with my lease ending, I wouldn't have even entertained the thought of living under his roof, but at least I could save money. All I had to do was pay for gas for the hour-long commute from Miami to Tampa on the days I had class. The more money I saved in Miami, meant the more money I'd have for my future in Cali.

Two weeks later.

It'd been a few weeks since I moved into the private first-floor suite in Rome's house. Everything had been smooth sailing. He ensured I had three meals a day approved by a prenatal nutritionist and prepared by a private chef. In return, I made sure to stay out of their way.

Late one night, I was on my way to the kitchen for something to wash down the gross prenatal vitamin when I witnessed Cash kiss Draya under the soft glow of the living room TV. The fact that she didn't immediately pull away told me it wasn't the first time that had happened. Part of me didn't blame her. Cash was easy on the eyes, but he was her husband's best friend. He was more than off-limits. I quietly stepped back, freezing, when the alarming sound of the floor creaked underneath me. They quickly pulled away from each other, and I hurried in the opposite direction down the hallway, praying no one saw me. I hadn't been in the lap of luxury long, and I wasn't ready to give it up. The last thing I needed was problems.

I woke up the following day to a gentle knock on my bedroom door. Hesitant, I entangled my body from the high thread count sheets and walked over to open it. Draya was standing on the other side with bright eyes.

"Did I wake you?" she asked.

I stretched while shaking my head. "No. Um, I was about to get up soon."

"I wanted to see if you wanted to join me at the spa later today."

"Are you sure?"

"Yeah. Shouldn't we get the elephant out of the room already and get to know each other? After all, you are carrying my son or daughter."

A ghost of a smile spread across my face. "Yeah, sure. Um, okay. I'll start getting ready now."

"Cool. I'll come to get you in like an hour," she declared before leaving.

She hadn't said more than two words to me since I moved in. Again, I made it my business to stay out of their way. All I wanted to do was lay low for the duration of the pregnancy and get the rest of my money when the time came. I wasn't trying to make friends or exchange Christmas cards with them when everything was said and done. But at the same time, I didn't know what would happen if I didn't accept.

We'd managed to make it through massages, facials, and manicures without having to speak to each other too much. It wasn't until we were getting pedicures that she decided to spark up a conversation.

"How are you doing at the house? All settled in?" Draya asked, looking up from the magazine she had her nose buried in.

"Yeah, I am."

"Do you have everything you need?"

"Yup, I'm good…."

She gave me what I assumed was her best attempt at small talk, but I would've preferred the silence.

"So, do you think you'll start dating, or would that be too awkward? Y'know, with the belly in all?" she randomly blurted out.

My brows snapped together as I shot her a puzzled look. "Um, I never thought about it."

"Rome would probably lose his mind if you went out on a date while pregnant."

"He's stricter than I thought he'd be about that meal prep shit. He's earnest about this baby."

"He's serious about you."

I snapped my neck in her direction. "W–what? Why would you say that?"

"He's attracted to you, Lira. You think I don't see that? I mean, he'd have to be blind not to be."

"Draya, you don't have to worry about Rome and me doing anything ever again. I made things very clear to him. This entire thing is a business deal to me. I don't want your man."

She studied me in silence for a few seconds, face blank and motionless. Then out of nowhere, a smile spread across her face. "I appreciate that."

"No problem. So, what's with you two anyway?"

"What do you mean?"

"Do you do what you did with me with, you know, other people?" I inquired.

"My husband and I...we have an understanding. If I want to have a little bedroom fun with someone other than him, he gets that."

"So, both of you can have sex with anyone you want? Like an open marriage?"

"As I said, we have an understanding. And it's not *anyone*. Not someone like Cash. No, Cash is like family, you know? More like a brother."

"Why are you telling me this?"

"I'm just saying...."

In the midst of her rambling, it clicked. It was my first time seeing her off her game. I knew better than to attack when she was weak. Confirmation that my presence bothered her was more than enough. To her, I was an extra set of eyes that could easily cramp her style.

"If you have something specific you wanna say to me, just go ahead, Draya."

"Look, Lira, I don't know what you thought you saw last night, but–"

"I didn't see anything."

"I thought I saw you in the–never mind. Rome is probably gonna kill me for keeping you hostage all day." She chuckled, trying to change the subject as quickly as she could.

"He needs to take a chill pill. I want French fries, and I'm not going home until I get them," I said, playing along.

As much as I wanted to tell her I didn't give a fuck about what she did or who she did it with, I let it slide. Peace was a frame of mind that I was determined to reside in.

"I could definitely go for some fries after this."

"Okay."

"Hey, um, at the risk of sounding overly insecure to my husband, I'd like to keep things between us girls, if you don't mind."

"Sure," I told her.

"Good," she said before leaning over to peck my lips. "I think we're going to get along just fine."

DRAYA

I could've killed Rome when I found out he went and offered the bitch that stole his money to carry his fuckin' kid. A kid that wasn't even mine was gonna be callin' me mommy. What kinda bullshit was that? I knew we said for better or worse, but what the fuck? With Lira around, I wasn't playing the main character in my own love story, and I wasn't about to let what Rome wanted, overshadow what I needed. Because I could barely stand to look at Rome, I had Cash putting in overtime. We'd been doing it like rabbits, but it was always casual, nothing heavy. I couldn't deal with anything more severe than what was currently going on in my life. I needed something to help take the edge off all the rage I had pent-up inside me, and he'd become the remedy. I found comfort in his tattoo-laced arms because it was easy, convenient even. It was always a decision I anticipated I would regret the morning after, but it'd been months, and that sunrise hadn't come yet.

"Mmm. You smell so fuckin' good," Cash purred as he grabbed my arm and pulled me inside the private hotel suite.

"Thanks, but I didn't come here to fuck," I informed him.

"You sure about that?" he asked, stroking the monster pressing against his joggers.

I stepped out of his grasp. "I'm serious, Cash. I came to talk."

"About?"

"We have to be careful, and when I say we, I mean you. No more feeling me up in the house and shit."

"Why not?"

"Because I think Lira saw us. I don't need her running behind me and telling Rome what she thinks she saw."

"Why would she do that?"

"I don't know, but I'm not trying to risk it! So just chill. We have to chill!"

"Fine. I'll try to keep my hands to myself," he said before circling his arms around my waist and letting his fingertips glide over my ass.

"Cash!" I protested, swatting his hands away from my body.

"You said I couldn't touch you at your crib. We ain't there, baby."

"What did I tell you about callin' me that?" I snapped.

A whizz of air expelled from his lips. "There you go. You sure your cranky ass don't want no dick? Let Daddy break you off real quick."

He bent me over the bed and towered over me from behind; my teeth sunk into my bottom lip before I flipped onto my back. I'd be lying if I said Cash wasn't a pleasure to look at. His milk chocolate skin dripped with tattoo ink from his neck to his sexy V-cut. He was of Black and Samoan descent with long, thick dreads and a thick dick to match. We'd been doing our thing for months in secret, and as much as I wanted to quit, I couldn't. His long dreads swung in my face as he climbed on top of me and placed kisses on my neck. "Cash, I don't think we…."

"You don't think we what?" he asked, continuing to place kisses down my chest while unbuttoning my blouse.

I sat up on my elbows. "Too much is going on underneath my roof."

"And now you wanna quit me? You can't get me hooked and take it from me, Dray. I can't have that."

"If we can't quit, we have to be more careful. No more slip-ups."

"You want me to keep it tight? I got you. I'd do anything for you, baby. You know that," he said before dropping between my thighs.

"Cash, you can't–oh shit," I panted, sucking in air through my teeth.

My protests were replaced by moans the second his tongue sliced across my tender flesh.

"You really do have to stop calling me that," I told him after the third round.

"What?"

"Baby. I'm not your baby. I'm just...Dray or Draya. Not baby," I reminded him.

"When you with me, you're my baby. I don't care what you say, Dray."

"You're going to make me regret this more than I already do," I warned him.

"How are things at home?" he asked, changing the subject.

"No change. Still as shitty as ever," I complained. "I feel invisible, and the baby isn't even here yet."

"How are things with Lira? Do you think she'll be a problem?"

"I don't know yet."

"What about Rome? He really wanna do this daddy shit?"

"He wants it more than anything, and I hate that about him," I confessed.

He shook his head in a swift arc. "For what it's worth, I still think that nigga Rome is trippin'. I would never choose another woman to bear my seed over you. I would never leave you out here feelin' like I didn't have your back. That's not what you do to someone you love."

I sighed as a tear slipped down my cheek, and I swiped it away with haste. "I'm sorry for the tears. I just wish it was him saying that instead of–"

"I love you, Dray!" he exclaimed.

I looked up at him. "Wait, are you serious right now?"

"Yeah, I'm serious. I'm in love with you, Draya."

"Love me, what do you mean you love me? Why would you fuck around and do something stupid like that?" I asserted, sitting up on my elbows.

"I know it wasn't supposed to happen, but I do."

"No. No! You can't love me, Cash. That wasn't a part of the arrangement between us!" I fumed while throwing on one article of clothing after another.

"Yeah, well, my heart says something different. Face it, Draya. I get you. I'm everything you love in a man and a lover. I'm smart, paid, and I've given you some of the best dick of your life. You said it yourself."

"I'm married, Cash! End of story!" I said, grabbing my purse. "I have to go."

"Don't go," he called out.

"I have to!"

"No, you don't. What can I do to convince you to stay? Listen, I–I didn't mean to freak you out, but I've been holding our secret in for months, Dray. You at least owe it to me to talk this out. Stay, please."

Cash reached out for me, and I drew away. "There's nothing to talk about, Cash! You made me curious. We explored it. Now somehow, in the midst of all that, you fell in love. I'm not here to validate your feelings, okay? I have to go! I can't be here right now."

I let out a frantic sigh as I raced to the door. I knew things would turn around to bite me in the ass, but I forged ahead anyway. Cash chased me to the door and placed his hand on mine when I touched the door handle.

"You think I wanna love you like this? You think I want to be doing this behind my best friend's back? Being with you fucks me up mentally and emotionally! Get over yourself, Draya, because if I could get over you, I swear to God I would," he growled before snatching his hand away from mine.

Instead of responding, I raced out of the hotel to my car. A full-blown panic attack had set in by the time I got inside. Hours ago, I was having fun. Hours ago, we were still a fling. Hours ago, I was living my best life. Cash had gone and ruined everything by falling in love. I already had enough going on. I didn't need to deal with his feelings on top of everything else. The second I walked through the front door, I made my way upstairs to the shower to erase the scent of Cash from my body and hopefully clear my head before I had to face Rome. Halfway through my shower, I heard the bathroom door open.

"Dray?" Rome called out.

"I'll be out in a minute," I responded.

Instead of acknowledging my response, he opened the shower door with no clothes on and stepped inside. Rome wrapped his arms around me and nuzzled his head in my neck and shoulder crevice.

"Are you okay, bae? You're shaking."

"I'm okay," I said as a tear slipped down my cheek.

"I love you above all else, Dray, remember that," he confirmed.

Another tear slipped down my cheek, instantly camouflaged by the water droplets on Rome's firm, wet chest. "I love you too."

I hugged him tightly, knowing the day would come when I'd have to reap what I sowed. Cash's confession meant there was no way I would be able to continue to have my cake and another cake, too, no matter how I sliced it.

ROME

Draya had been gone for a couple of days for her sister's wedding. I stayed behind to make some money moves and re-up on product with Baby and Cash. After finishing up everything I needed to do, I had the afternoon to myself and decided to relax at the house. Relaxing was something I hardly ever did unless I was fuckin'. I stepped out of the shower soaking wet and swiped my phone off the bed to order some Thai food. Lira instantly came to mind, and I figured I'd see if she wanted anything before placing my order. I threw on some clothes and headed down to the guest quarters on the main floor where Lira was staying. My fist collided with the door as I waited for her to answer. She pulled the door open seconds later and flashed her tired eyes up at mine. My eyes deviated from hers straight down to her small but noticeable baby bump.

"Yeah?" she asked.

"I was about to order some Thai. You want anything?"

93

She shook her head. "No. I don't feel the best right now."

"What's wrong? And did you eat today?"

"I'm just a little congested, and my nose is stuffy. And no, nothing but water."

"You need to eat, Lira. What do you want me to order you?"

"I told you I'm not hungry."

"I don't care if I have to sit you down and feed you myself; you're gonna eat. You're carrying my baby."

She pushed an exhale past her lips. "Fine. Whatever. I'll eat."

"What do you want?"

"Wonton soup, and maybe some tea if you have any."

"Bet. I'll bring it to you when it gets here."

I headed into the kitchen to see if we had any tea and to place the food order. I decided to run out and pick up the food and a few more things since we didn't have any tea. Shuffling down the hall, I went back to Lira's door and knocked again to let her know I was leaving.

"We're out of tea. I'm gonna run out and get you some stuff and pick up the food. You need anything else?"

"Ice cream."

"What?"

"I know it sounds random, but I have a taste for ice cream."

"What kind?"

"I don't know."

I sucked my teeth. "You wanna ride with me then? I'll take you to get some after picking up the food and stuff."

"Okay. Let me get dressed. I'll see you in a few minutes."

Ten minutes later, she met me in the kitchen wearing a simple white tank top and gray sweatpants with her tiny baby bump poking out, which made me catch my breath in my throat. Her hair was swept up into a high curly bun, and I couldn't help but stare. She looked breathtaking with no effort at all.

"Are you just going to stand there and gawk?"

"Yes," I admitted without shame or stutter.

"Well, don't. You look stupid, and I look terrible. Pick up your tongue before you step on it, and let's go get my ice cream," she joked.

When we arrived at the ice cream shop, she hurried inside to get to the counter. "There are like four million flavor combinations here. How will I ever choose?" she pondered.

Laughter bubbled in my throat as my phone rang. I looked down to see Draya's name across the screen and handed Lira a twenty-dollar bill before I swiped to answer.

"Hey, Dray," I answered before stepping away. "What's up?"

"Nothing, I was just checking in on you to see how you're doing."

"I'm good. How are things with your family? You tell 'em I said what's up?"

"Yeah, I did, and it's cool. All the little festivities lined up for the families are cute or whatever. Meet and greets, and brunch, and all that. Shanti is keeping me busy, I'll tell you that."

"Yeah, I bet."

"Did you get everything you needed done?"

"Yeah, I'm out picking up something to eat now."

"Okay."

"I'm not gon' keep you from your family, bae. I'll talk to you later, okay?"

"Okay, baby."

I hung up when Lira made her way back to the car, and we got inside. "Everything good?" she asked me.

"Yeah. What flavor did you end up getting?" I inquired, eyeing the three different scoops on top of her large waffle cone.

"One scoop is cake batter ice cream with Oreos, the second is chocolate ice cream with brownie chunks, and the third is chocolate-dipped strawberry ice cream with red velvet cake."

"Damn. It's like a sea of ice cream."

"You mean an island of pure dairy bliss," she corrected me. "You know you want some."

"You gon' let me get a bite?" I asked.

"I guess."

She offered it to me, and I licked the top section while looking into her eyes. "Damn, it is good as hell."

She quirked her lips before propping her feet up on the dash. "Told you."

I would've told her to put her feet down if she had been anybody else, but I let it slide. Instead, I pulled them off and put them on my lap to rub them.

"What do you think you're doing?" she asked.

"Does it feel good?"

"It feels amazing, but that's not the point."

"Then. let me do my thing and give me another taste."

"Of what?" she asked.

My lips squirmed to the side. "Your ice cream, girl."

"Here," she said, sitting up to let me taste the second scoop.

"Damn, I like that layer even more than the first one."

"It only gets better the further you go down," she confirmed.

My eyes galloped over to her with the right side of my mouth lifted in a smirk. "Yo, stop playin' with me."

"I don't know what you're talking about."

"Your ass knows exactly what I'm talkin' about."

Laughter drifted from her throat as she continued to lick her ice cream. "Mmhm."

I started the engine and put the car in gear. "You gotta plan, y'know, for after the baby comes?"

"It's funny you ask because I've been thinking a lot about what I was going to do post-birth. This kid's been good to me so far, but I don't know what my body will look like when all this is over. But if I don't have too many scars or stretch marks, I'm seriously considering lining up dance auditions for an NBA dance team or something on the West Coast," she answered.

My eyebrows lifted. "The West Coast?" I asked, voicing my surprise.

"Yeah."

"Why so far?"

She shrugged her lean shoulders. "I've never been, and I need a fresh start. I figure what better way to start fresh than to move across the country?"

"You could up and leave like that knowing you got a kid out there?"

She bobbed her head. "Yeah. Especially when it won't be *my* kid. It'll be yours, remember? So, after I get this degree, there will be nothing left for me in Miami. So, yeah, leaving is the plan."

I let the conversation hang where it was, getting soaked up in my own thoughts for a second before she spoke up again.

"Trust me, when all this is over, you're gonna want your space from me. If not you, then definitely Draya. Nobody needs the creepy birth mom hanging around in the background. I'd probably only do more harm than good anyway."

"Why do you think that?"

"What role model did I have growing up? I had two druggie parents who cared more about crack than the kid they made. I was in and out of foster care for most of my childhood. I'm the last thing this kid needs."

"Anybody can learn from anybody, and anybody can teach anybody something, too," I informed her.

"Look at you. Got the dad advice at the ready." She uttered a soft laugh before gripping the center console. "Whoa."

"What is it? Are you okay?"

"Everything is fine; it's just—I think I felt the baby kick."

"Wow? Can I feel it—I mean, if it's not too awkward for you..."

"You've seen me naked once, and now I'm carrying your baby, Rome. We're past the point of awkwardness. It's fine. Put your hand right here," she directed, guiding my hand to her stomach. "There it goes again. Did you feel it?"

"No."

"Keep talking. I felt it when you were talking."

"Can it hear me?"

"I don't know, but keep talking anyway," she told me.

"What do you want me to say?"

"Don't think so hard. Say anything." She chuckled.

"Nice weather we're having, huh?"

Lira let out a mouthful of laughter. "Did you feel it that time?"

"I think I may have felt a little something. It was faint, but it was there. That's pretty crazy."

"I know, right. Like something is living and moving around inside me."

"A whole life," I replied.

"Can I tell you a secret?"

"What?"

"You have to promise not to judge me because it's heavy. And if you're not ready for heavy, let me know now, and I'll understand. Because once I say it, it's out there, and I can't take it back."

"Say it, Lira."

"I think I'm falling in love with this baby, and I'm terrified."

I turned to look at her thoroughly. "Why?"

"Why am I falling in love, or why am I terrified?"

"Both."

"Because this isn't real, Rome. None of this is real."

"It's real to me."

She shook her head before redirecting her attention out of the window. "You don't get it."

"Then explain it to me."

"Look, I know this all sounds crazy because I went into this as a job. You and Draya, you paid me to do a job. And I'm thankful for the money, I am. If it weren't for that, I wouldn't have been able to enroll back in school so quickly. In the beginning, I looked at this entire pregnancy as the worst thing that could've ever happened to me, and I'm grateful for the moment this baby comes out of me, and I can have my life back because all my life it's only ever been me. But then, there are these moments when you look at me the way you're looking at me right now, and I find myself daydreaming about baby names, and whose features they'll have, or what their room will look like, and then I remember that I don't get to make any of those decisions, Rome. I don't get the picture-perfect family. I don't get the mommy firsts or the long, exhausting nights. I don't get to roll over and look at you at two o'clock in the morning, sleep-deprived and all, and tell you it's your turn to get the baby. I guess what I'm trying to say is that being here with you feels so damn good, but it's driving me crazy because I know it all has an expiration date."

Her honesty rendered me speechless for a few seconds. When I parted my lips to speak, only two words fell out. "I'm sorry."

"For what?"

"For everything."

"What do you mean?"

"I never took the time to ask you if you wanted any of this. It's like, I wanted it so bad that I ain't give a fuck if I forced motherhood on you or not, and I'm sorry for that."

"Why do you want this baby so bad, Rome?"

I paused, contemplating whether I was comfortable with letting words I'd never spoken aloud hit her ears. "She was pregnant when she died," I confided.

"Who?"

"Jhene."

Lira's eyes bugged at the news. "What? I—I didn't know that."

"Nobody did. It was early. We were the only ones who knew about it. We made plans to tell our families when she made it through the first trimester, but...yeah."

"What happened that night, if you don't mind me asking?"

"Jevan never told you?"

She shook her head. "He only said you made some enemies, and they shot up your car with her inside, outside of the club."

I slowly bobbed my head. "I bought a new car for my birthday. We were out that night because I wanted to show it off. A polar white Mercedes AMG four-door coupe. Everything on it was custom. I'm talkin' chrome accents on the exterior, red leather on the interior, panorama roof, an engine that went from zero to sixty in four seconds, heated steering wheel, you name it. We'd been going back and forth about when I was gon' let her drive it. There was a thunderstorm earlier that night, and there were big puddles throughout the parking lot. Jhene didn't want to get her feet wet. She was funny like that. So, I made sure to have the valet park the car. We went inside. We had a good time. We were happy. When we left, we were standing outside waiting for the car to be brought around when Cash called me back inside. I told her to come with me, I did, but she told me she'd be okay.

I never should've gone back inside. It was a second. I was gone for a second. The gunshots rang so loud, I heard them over the music inside. I ran outside to see Jhene's blood splattered all over the dash. A couple of young niggas trying to make a name for themselves thought it would be cool to catch me slippin'. They pulled up on my car and shot it up, thinking I was inside. She'd gotten in the driver's seat to spite me. She always loved to piss me off. She knew I always drove when we were out because I never trusted niggas. I always drove, and she got in the driver's seat and took bullets for me. The worst part of it all is that I lost two lives that night. I had a different life planned for us, and when it was all taken away from me in the blink of an eye, I thought I'd never recover. This baby is my second chance."

Lira reached out and placed her hand on mine. "Rome, I'm sorry. I get it now."

"Don't be. It was a long time ago. You wanted an answer, and you got one," I paused, "damn."

"What?"

I exhaled. "You're the first person I ever told that shit to."

"Really? No one knows?"

"No."

"Not even Draya?"

"Not Draya, not my brothers, and not even Cash."

"Well, thank you for sharing it with me."

"You're welcome."

"Hey, um…you said you had a different life planned out. What did you envision? Like, what was your dream?" she asked.

"Growing up, I didn't have both parents all the time. Our father got deported back to Jamaica when we were kids, and our mom worked two jobs trying to keep food on the table for all three of us and wait for our father to send money over every month. After losing Jhene, I never really spent too much time thinking about being a father or what that meant until you. Kids were never in the cards for Draya and me until you. Now not a day goes by that I don't think about little shit like passing down the remedy of cough syrup and grape soda that our mother used to make us whenever we were sick to help the medicine go down easier, you know? I never saw myself being that guy, but now it's the only guy I wanna be," I admitted.

"Hearing you talk like that makes me happy," she told me.

"Why?"

"I mean, carrying a baby is one thing, but being a mother is something else. Who knows what type of mother I'd be? So at least having you for a father gives this baby a fighting chance."

"My dad was a great father when he was around, but I don't know what type of father I'll be either. I'm not sayin' it's gon' be easy, but it'll be worth it."

"Yeah, and at least it sounds like you had a decent family as a kid. I grew up in and out of foster care for the greater part of my childhood. The days were long, and the nights were even longer. But as far back as I can remember, dancing has always been my bliss. I could barely stand still at any given moment like I was always dancing to a beat that no one could hear. It was the only thing that could take me out of the shitty situation I was living in. So naturally, I wanted to dance for the rest of my life, but tuition seemed like it would put a stop to that before I could finish my studies."

"You went to school for dance?"

"I majored in dance performance with a concentration in modern dance. I only needed a few more classes to graduate before I dropped out three years ago."

"Damn, why didn't you finish?"

"Life. I got caught up and missed some important assignments in my studio electives during my last year, which made me lose my scholarship. Once that happened, I couldn't afford to pay for school and my bills, so I dropped."

"Damn, you were that close?"

She scoffed. "Yup. It's one of my biggest regrets."

"Really?"

"How would you feel if you fumbled the ball with only four months left?"

I agreed. "I guess you're right. But you're back in now, right?"

"Yeah, I am. Thanks to you. It only took me getting knocked up to make me wanna get my shit together." She said with a sweet laugh on her lips. "I guess it's all a blessing in disguise somehow, I don't know. Maybe that's just what people say to make themselves feel better."

"What do you want to do after you get settled in Cali?"

"Well, the goal is to land a job within six months of graduating, but my dream is to one day…you know what, never mind."

"Nah, tell me."

She shook her head. "It's stupid. It'll never happen."

"What is it?"

She nervously shook her head and started talking with her hands a bit. "I have this stupid dream. I've had it since I was a kid. So, one day I want to open up my own dance academy to have kids who feel like they have nowhere to go come and be able to learn and express themselves creatively through dance. That's all I ever wanted to do when I was young. I was never good at expressing how I felt through my own words, but I could always express everything on my mind through someone else's."

"That's dope. I could see that happening for you."

Her shoulders speedily rose and fell. "Who knows, maybe one day."

"What if the baby was still in your life? Would you still want to open up your school?"

"What do you mean? Like, actually raising it?"

"Yeah."

"I–I don't know. I never had anybody pass anything down to me, so I think if I were to do it, it would be dope to have something to pass down to the baby, you know?"

"Yeah."

"Why'd you ask that?"

"You told me you've been thinking about it."

"Yeah, but have you?"

I glanced over at her while chewing my bottom lip. Truthfully, I was conflicted. All I'd ever cared about from the moment I found out Lira was carrying my baby was becoming a father and keeping some link to her, directly or indirectly. I was so close to getting what I wanted that I could taste it, but I'd be lying if I said I hadn't envisioned what life would be like raising my baby with its biological mother.

"If I was…what would that mean?" I asked her.

A sigh leaked from her lungs. "I don't know, Rome. You tell me."

"I can't do that right now, Lira. You know that."

"If you're having doubts, even the slightest bit, you need to tell me, Rome."

"What would that change? I'm still married," I reminded her.

"You're right. You are, and I don't want to overstep any boundaries by saying this because I know you'll be a good father; I—I'd be lying to you if I said I wasn't thinking a lot about this baby and what will happen after its born, especially with Draya."

"What about her?"

"Does she seem a bit off to you?"

"In what way?"

"I don't know. Everything seems like one big game of pretend to her while I'm the one over here with leg spasms and backaches every other day. I want to make sure that her priorities are right when the baby gets here and it's time to be parents."

"The baby will be fine. And listen, when it comes to Dray, I know how off the cuff she can seem. She moves to the beat of her own drum, but she's the most nurturing person I know. She's a giver. She will give this baby everything she has to offer. There's no doubt in my mind about that, and there shouldn't be any doubt in yours."

"But there are doubts. We both made that very clear."

"I don't have all the answers. I wish I did, but I don't," I told her as we pulled into the driveway.

"Yeah, neither do I." She drove out a harsh sigh before pulling on the latch to open the door.

I hopped out to catch up with her and wrapped my arms around her waist, cradling her stomach in my palms. "Lira."

She spun around to face me. "Get off me, Rome. I don't wanna talk anymore. I will find out the sex of the baby at my appointment in a few days. Other than that, we don't need to speak."

"I'm sorry, okay? Sometimes I wish all this shit was different, but it's not. All I know is that being here with you does somethin' to me, and I don't want to lose it. As selfish as it sounds, I don't."

"The baby just kicked again," she announced, grabbing my hand.

She placed my hand against her skin, and I rested my forehead against hers. We stood there, feeling the life we created together move around inside her while soaking in the silence. I felt her heartbeat throbbing through her chest cavity.

"I make you nervous?" I whispered.

She shrugged. "Apparently."

I lifted her chin so she could look me in the eyes. "You're carryin' my seed, Lira. You ain't never gotta be scared of me."

She'd seen what I was capable of firsthand, but she was the mother of my child, and I would never let anything happen to her. Against all logic, I pulled her lips onto mine so gently that it was barely a kiss at all at first. I held onto her waist, pressing my lips to her temple while sinking further into the moment and deepening the entanglement of our heartstrings.

DRAYA

I TOSSED MY CUSTOM LOUIS VUITTON SUITCASE ONTO THE PLUSH, KING-sized hotel bed before stepping over to the window to catch the perfect view of the Philadelphia skyline right from the privacy of my suite. My baby sister, Ashanti, was getting married to her college sweetheart in his hometown, so I flew in on Thursday for the weekend's festivities. After spending the first two nights in a drunken stupor with the bride and the rest of her bridesmaids, I woke up with a hellacious hangover the morning of the wedding.

"How are you feeling?" Shanti asked me as the makeup artist made me come alive by hiding the bags under my eyes.

"No change," I mumbled, sipping from the bottle of ginger ale I was clutching.

"Please tell me you're not going to be walking down the aisle with your bouquet in a barf bag, Dray!" she whined.

"No. I promise I'll get it together. I need to get some food in my system."

"We got some snacks in the other suite. What do you want? We got a lil' bit of everything in there."

"I'll go take a look," I told her.

Once my makeup and mink lash application was complete, I got up to go to the other suite to put something on my stomach. Shanti wasn't lying about the spread. There were two fruit trays lined with everything from pineapples and strawberries to melons and grapes. There were fried chicken strips, mini-Belgian waffles, champagne and orange juice for mimosas, and a platter full of a dozen doughnuts. As good as everything looked, the longer I stayed in the room, the more nauseous I became. I hurried away from the food and slammed the bathroom door behind me. I heaved over the toilet bowl, spilling my insides. After flushing and rinsing out my mouth, I opened the door to see Shanti standing there with her arms folded across her chest.

She side-eyed me. "Mmmm."

"What?"

"Maybe you should take a pregnancy test."

"Maybe your mama should take a pregnancy test! Don't wish that shit on me!" I scolded.

"Bitch, she yo mama too!" Shanti giggled.

"No, but for real. Why would you say that?"

"You been fuckin'?"

"Is the sky blue?" I asked back.

"Then it ain't that farfetched, is it?"

I smacked my lips. "Too bad I'm fresh out of sticks to pee on."

"That's what family is for. I got one in my bag you can take right now."

"Bitch, you carryin' around pregnancy tests in your bag like Queen Bey carries hot sauce in hers?" I asked with a slight chuckle slipping past my lips.

"Always be prepared! I'll be right back."

"I'm not pregnant, Shanti! This is a waste of time!"

"We'll see, Dray."

"Bitch, you jinxed me!" I screamed, seeing the plus sign on the test a few minutes later.

"Oh my God! This is the best wedding present you could've ever given me, Dray! I'm gonna be an auntie! Hey Pooh! It's your Auntie Shanti!" she cooed at my abdomen.

"Chill, Shanti!"

"Excuse me for being excited. I bet Rome is going to be so happy. My brother-in-law is gonna be a great dad! I'm so mad he couldn't be here this weekend!"

"I know."

"Are you gonna tell him as soon as you get home? Oh my God, how are you gonna say it? Are you gonna surprise him with something special or blurt it out as soon as you walk through the front door?"

"Can you chill with the twenty-one questions? I'm still in shock, for one. Two, today is your day. I don't wanna talk about anything have to do with me or this baby," I told her.

I may have put a damper on her parade, but she needed to take a chill pill. As excited as she was about becoming an auntie, I was too busy swept up in who the father was. It could've easily been Rome or Cash's baby, and if it were the latter, we'd all be fucked.

On the drive home from the airport, I built up the nerve to call my husband and tell him the news. The phone rang three times before I heard his familiar baritone voice on the other end.

"You just landed, beautiful?" he asked.

"Yeah. I got my bag, and I'm in the car and on my way home to you." I smiled.

"Cool. Are you hungry? You want me to order somethin' and have it delivered by the time you get here?"

"Eh, I don't have much of an appetite. Haven't had much of one for the better half of the weekend," I confessed.

"What's wrong? You caught a stomach bug or somethin' while you were up there?"

"More like a baby…." I muttered.

"What?"

"I'm pregnant, Rome."

The line fell silent for a few seconds before he replied. "Are you serious?"

"Y–yeah."

"How do you feel about that, Dray?"

"I–I don't know," I admitted, swiping a tear from my eyes.

"Whatever you wanna do, I'm with you."

I bobbed my head. "I know you are. You're so good to me, baby."

"We'll talk about it more when you get home, okay? How far away are you?"

"Like twenty minutes."

"Bet. I'll see you in a minute."

"Rome."

"Yeah, Dray?"

"I love you."

"I love you, too," he replied before ending the call.

I released a stifled breath while redirecting my focus on the road ahead of me. Rome was a remarkable man from the top of his head to the soles of his feet. It seemed like we'd gone from one maybe baby to a potential family of four in the blink of an eye, and the ball was in my court on whether we stayed that way. There was no way Cash could find out that the baby I was carrying could potentially be his, especially knowing how he felt about me. He'd get too attached and ruin everything. I cursed myself for not cutting things off when he confessed his feelings for me months prior, but the dick was good and convenient whenever I needed to blow off some steam. If Rome was going to stand behind me and be the father I knew he could be to our baby, I would do the right thing and raise my baby with my man. Besides, if I could agree to raise a baby that he fathered with another woman, he could be the father of his best friend's son.

ROME

I'D BEEN TRYING TO KEEP MY FEELINGS FOR LIRA AT BAY, BUT THE weekend we spent together only strengthened them. Draya's surprise pregnancy announcement threw me for a loop and gave me the reality check I didn't know I needed. The phone pressed against my ear, and I heard it ring before Chief picked up.

"Yo, you busy?" I asked. "Some shit is weighing on me, and I gotta tell somebody."

"What is it?" Chief asked through the receiver.

"Dray's pregnant," I announced.

"Oh shit. And how far along is your other baby mama?"

"She's somewhere in her second trimester," I answered.

"Damn, you about to have a set of project twins, huh? How you feel about that?"

"Don't talk about your nieces or nephews like that. I'm being serious. I don't know what to do. I can't be upset about having a child with my wife, right?"

"I mean, you can, but what kinda man would that make you?" he asked.

"I'm lowkey happy about expanding my family. I didn't think it would happen this soon or like this, but I'm okay with it."

"There was a time not too long ago when you were callin' me the father of the year and shit, and now look at you."

I chuckled. "Shut up, man. I hope it's as easy as you make it seem."

"It's anything but easy, and it definitely won't be with two baby mamas."

"Two kids, one mother," I corrected him.

"That's right, my bad. So, question."

"Yeah?"

"You got Lira carrying your seed, Draya carrying the other. You say you're cool with the shit, but why is there so much conflict in your voice?" he queried.

The admission of guilt rolled off my tongue with ease. "I'd be lying if I said I didn't want both."

Chief scoffed. "You always did wanna have your cake and another cake, too."

"This shit is different."

"It's messy, and you know it. It was one thing to fuck another woman; y'all do whatever you want; I'm not judging. But at the end of the day, you are the one that made those vows to Draya. You already know what you should do; I ain't gotta say it."

Chief's words stuck with me until Draya walked through the front door. I decided to put my focus back on the number one woman in my life, Draya. I promised myself I would never cross the line with Lira again.

"Hey, bae," Draya greeted me with a smile.

I pulled her into my arms, engulfing her with all the love I had in me. "Hey, Dray."

I removed her bags from the car and put them upstairs while she took a shower. After throwing on something more comfortable, she crawled into my lap and looked up at me. "I think we should tell Lira."

"Are you sure you wanna say something right now?" I asked.

"Is there a reason you don't want her to know?"

"No."

"Then, I'm positive," she assured me.

"Okay, then let's go."

The two of us stepped up to Lira's door and knocked. The moment she opened it, I took one look at her face, and the best kind of frustration coursed through me. I clenched my fists. She stared us both in the face with confusion etched across hers.

I spoke first. "We have something to tell you."

"About what?"

Draya started. "Well, it's kind of early, but we wanted to tell you together."

"Tell me what?" she asked, getting more impatient by the second.

"I'm pregnant!" Draya blurted out.

I watched Lira's eyelids stretch wide as if her heart had just been flushed to her feet. "Y—you're what?" she asked.

ROME'S EYES CARVED INTO ME. "SHE'S PREGNANT, LIRA. DRAYA'S pregnant."

My breath halted when those words spilled from Rome's stupid mouth like bombs to my heart. I parted my lips to let a bitter *congratulations* roll off my tongue while plastering a strained smile across my face.

"Thanks," he replied, trying his hardest not to perch his eyes on me any longer.

"Yeah, thanks," Draya repeated.

"You two will have your hands full in a few months."

"We can handle it, right bae?" Draya asked, turning her attention to Rome.

He nodded. "Of course, we can."

"Well, we'll let you get back to what you were doing," Draya added.

"Sure, thanks. Congratulations again. That's great news for you two," I told them.

When the door closed, separating me from them, the fake smile I'd plastered across my face instantly melted off. I was astronomically crushed on the inside. I'd gone from never wanting him to touch me again to yearning for it after the kiss we shared, and it was all for nothing. Feeling foolish, I marched into the bathroom to splash some cold water on my face. I was ashamed that I even let the thought of us being anything more than what we were, play out in my mind. I could've sworn I felt something between us, but none of that mattered anymore. My heart had to accept what my mind already knew. Rome was married, and he'd never leave his wife for me.

"Silly girl," I sighed, staring at my reflection as a tear slipped down my cheek, "what did you expect?"

Feeling heartbroken and played, I crawled into bed and tried to blame the reason behind my emotional unraveling on my raging hormones.

Later that night, I made my way into the kitchen for a bottle of water and a snack before bed. Instead of flipping on the light, I headed straight for the fridge and let the light illuminate the space around me. Seconds later, all the lights in the kitchen lit up, placing Rome and me in close, unwanted contact.

"It's past midnight. Why are you still up?" he asked.

Instead of telling him the truth, I'd been drowning in an ocean of tissues and couldn't sleep after hearing the news of his second bouncing bundle of joy, I shrugged. "I'm becoming an insomniac. This is my new normal. Besides, I like being the only one awake sometimes. Everything is so peaceful when everyone is asleep."

"Mmm. I'm like that, too."

"Okay," I said before dipping my head back inside the fridge.

"Hey, uh, you good?" he asked.

"What?" I retorted, refusing to look at him.

"You know, with the news about the baby."

I snapped my eyes at him while my shoulders shrugged. "How else am I supposed to feel?"

"I don't know. You tell me."

I sucked my teeth while wielding my most cutting glare. "Can we not do this shit, Rome? We don't have to do this. We don't have to do any of this."

"What are you talking about?"

"You know exactly what the fuck I'm talking about! Are you trying to play me right now?" I quizzed, raising my voice.

"No, I'm not."

"So just stop. Because again, we don't have to do this. You don't owe me shit. Go out and have all the fuckin' babies you want!"

He stiffened his gaze. "What do you want me to do? I didn't plan for any of this to happen. Not you, and not her either."

"Yeah, well, here we all are. One big, baby-making factory. And to answer your question, I want you to own your shit and stop making me feel like I'm the only one who felt something between us this past weekend!"

"Lower your voice!" he hissed before pinching his lips together.

"You and I–"

"Lira!" he thundered before compressing his jaw.

I pushed out a heavy exhale. "You and I both know it was more than just this baby," I whispered.

"And what if it was?"

My eyes burned fury hot. "Thanks for your honesty. I know everything I need to know about you now."

"And what's that?"

"That I'd have to be a mothafuckin' fool to give my heart to you," I remarked before storming out.

DRAYA

THE DAY OF MY EIGHT-WEEK DOCTOR APPOINTMENT HAD FINALLY rolled around. After weeks of trying to wrap my head around having a life inside me, trying to figure out how I would handle Cash when he found out, and letting Rome cater to my every beck and call for a baby that may not have been his, Rome and I walked into my appointment hand-in-hand.

"You okay?" he asked.

"I need everything to go okay. It's not like I know what to expect," I confided in him.

He rubbed the back of my hand. "Everything is gonna be fine, baby."

After a twenty-minute wait, I left Rome behind in the waiting room as the ultrasound tech took me back to do my ultrasound. The silence was awkward as I lay on the small bed and let her insert the long wand inside my lady parts. Once her job was done, she simply looked at me. "The doctor will share your results."

"That's it?" I asked, sitting up on my elbows, confused.

"Yes. I'll be on the other side of the door while you redress, then I'll take you to your exam room."

"O–okay."

She led me back into the waiting area so that Rome could come back to the exam room with me. There was a knock on the door before my doctor and two nurses spoke with us. There was a somber feeling that crept into the small room with them. One look in her broken-hearted eyes, and I knew something was wrong.

"What's wrong?" I asked nervously.

Dr. Palmer put the file down on the counter's edge and looked at Rome and me. "I don't want to scare you, but it doesn't look good."

"What do you mean? What doesn't look good?" Rome inquired.

"The ultrasound showed that the baby's growth isn't where it should be for eight weeks gestation," she confirmed.

"What does that mean?"

"It means that there's a possibility that the fetus has stopped growing."

A frown etched into the side of my mouth. "You mean like, I'm having a miscarriage?"

"There's also a possibility that the dates are off, and we're too early right now. I want the nurses to do some bloodwork today to check your levels."

I shot her a confused look. "B–but I've been sick. Nauseous and throwing up almost every day for weeks!"

"Again, I don't want to get you too worked up right now. All I want you to do today is go home, kick your feet up, and rest. I'll have you come back in a couple of days for more bloodwork to compare your levels. If they continue to decrease, then–"

"Then what? That's it? It's over?" Rome interjected.

She took her eyes to the ground before responding. "Yes."

"No! No!" I repeated, throwing up my hand. "I want a second opinion. Maybe that tech didn't know how to do her job!"

"I understand you're upset, Draya; I do. The last thing I want to do is scare you, but I wouldn't be doing my job if I wasn't upfront with you about what's going on."

"If my baby is dead, why aren't I bleeding?" I snapped coldly, knowing there had to be some mistake.

"If the fetus has stopped growing, then sometimes it takes our bodies a little longer to realize what's going on."

"And if I never start to bleed?" I asked, feeling defeated.

"You have a couple of options."

"What are they?" Rome asked. "I want her to be comfortable."

"Well, there is an outpatient procedure we can do to remove the fetal tissue, or if you'd prefer to pass the fetus in the privacy of your own home, there's a pill," she informed us.

"But again, all I want you to do today is go home and rest. You don't have to make any decisions today. I'll see you in a few days."

The rounds of bloodwork and a second ultrasound proved the baby had stopped growing weeks earlier, deflating the last bit of hope I had left. I opted to take the pill at home with Rome by my side. Rome spent the next week doing everything for me. From foot rubs to washing my hair, he'd never been more attentive. He'd been at my every beck and call, going out of his way to make sure I was comfortable and had everything I needed while I allowed my body to heal from the miscarriage.

I would've liked to say losing the baby brought us closer, but my hormones had gotten the better of me. Lira's belly seemed to be growing by the second. I could barely look at her. She was a constant reminder that I was sadder than I thought about losing my baby. One night before bed, I was lying in the middle of the bed waiting for Rome to come out of the shower.

"I know what I want," I blurted out when he stepped out of the bathroom.

"What?" he asked, slicking his hair into a ponytail.

"Lira has to move out."

A groove slashed across his forehead. "What? I thought we agreed she'd stay here until the baby was born."

"I know what we agreed on, and I know what I said, but you're not listening to me right now, Rome! She has to go!"

"Why?"

"Because every time I look at Lira, I get physically fucking ill!" I outpoured in rage.

Empathy whooshed from his lungs. "You just need time to heal, mentally and physically, that's all."

"Why don't you hear me when I say that she has to go for me to heal? I don't need a constant reminder of what my body couldn't do around my house!"

"If it's what you want, I'll talk to her."

"It is what I want. I never wanted to be a mother, y'know? And then that fucking stick turned pink! And now, I–I feel empty. I want to give you something and now I can't. I was finally starting to wrap my head around this whole baby thing, and now this? I feel like I disappointed you," I confessed.

Rome walked over to the bed to look me in the eyes closely. "Never. We can make another baby whenever you're ready, Dray."

"You say that, and it registers in my brain. And I–I wanna believe it, but I can't."

"Why not?"

"Because we don't have time! People will see us with this new baby out of nowhere in a few months, and I think it'll be better if we pretend like I'm pregnant."

"What?" he questioned.

"I don't want to tell anybody I lost the baby."

"Who all knows now besides Lira and us?"

"My sister."

"Does she know Lira's pregnant?"

"No! No one can know about her!"

Rome shook his head. "Baby, I love you, I do. But, this is crazy, Dray, even for you."

"We can do this!"

"No, we can't. Lira is in her second trimester by now. It would never work. People will know," he declared while shaking his head in protest.

I sat up. "Think about it, baby. The only person in my family that knows right now is my sister, and I already swore that bitch to secrecy. The bridesmaids dress I wore at her wedding was super flowy and didn't hug my curves. I could've easily been four or so months pregnant, and no one would even know."

"And what happens when the baby comes months earlier than your family thinks?"

"Babies come early all the time, don't they?"

The skepticism was still written across his face when he looked at me. I spoke up again. "Baby, I need this. Please."

He bobbed his head before crawling onto the bed and pulling me into a hug. "I'll talk to her tomorrow."

AFTER FINDING OUT THE SEX OF THE BABY AT MY DOCTOR'S appointment, I headed back to the house, debating whether to share the news. The right thing would've been to tell both Draya and Rome together, but after finding out about her miscarriage, I made double sure to stay out of her way. I didn't want to be insensitive. I immediately felt terrible about the jealousy I felt when the news of her pregnancy first hit my ears. I'd made sure to keep my distance from Rome, too. After our last conversation, I'd been avoiding the chance to be alone with him again. Not for any reason. Not for any amount of time, but withholding the information about the sex of *his* baby was too petty.

Ever since the kiss, I never knew I wanted to happen, I'd been all caught up in my feelings and couldn't get him off my mind. Knowing I couldn't change anything between us made me more frustrated than anything. Hating him was more exhausting than the alternative. Despite my efforts to avoid him, the moment I walked through the front door, I saw him passing through to the kitchen. He stopped when he saw me and doubled back. Every time I saw him, it was like he sent my heart on a rollercoaster ride.

He was the first to speak. "Hey."

"Hey..."

"There's something I need to talk to you about."

"What is it?" I quizzed.

"You have to move out."

Creases amassed on my forehead. "What? I thought I was staying here until I had the baby. That's what we agreed on."

"I know what we agreed on, Lira, but I can't take the unbalance in my home. I can't have it where I lay my head at night."

"So, where do I go?"

"I got you an apartment set up in a new complex twenty minutes from here, so I can check in on you whenever I desire. Plus, it's close to the hospital where you'll be delivering. It's fully furnished, on the first floor, so as you continue to get bigger, you won't have to worry about any stairs."

"Seems like you've thought of everything, huh?"

"Lira, I-"

"And I don't need you checking in on me. Despite what you may think, I am completely capable of taking care of myself."

"We've talked about this, and we agreed that-"

"If you can make changes to the agreement, so can I!"

A sigh blasted from his lungs. "I had all your things packed when you were out, and there's a-"

I folded my arms across my racing chest. "This was Draya's doing, right?"

"This doesn't have shit to do with her."

"Bullshit, Rome!" I spat. "She's always hated that I'm pregnant with your baby, and she hates me even more because of what happened to her. Admit it! And you know she doesn't want shit to do with this baby when it gets here! The only reason she's going along with any of this is because of you! She doesn't want to lose you! Even if she doesn't fuckin' deserve you!" I fumed, feelings flying out of my mouth.

His lips twisted into a snarl. "Like I was saying, there's a car waiting for you outside. I'll check in on you soon, give you some time to settle in."

I scoffed. "Yeah, okay. No, you're right about the unbalance. Because everything underneath this roof is unbalanced as fuck, and you don't even see it! So, yeah! I'm happy to go! The space will do everyone some good. Thanks for packing my shit!"

More vexed than I ever thought I'd be, I spun on my heels and headed back toward the door. Before storming out, I dug inside my purse and tossed the ultrasound pictures from my appointment at him. "Oh, and by the way, it's a fuckin' boy!" I spat before slamming the door behind me.

ROME

I SWIPED UP THE ROLL OF ULTRASOUND PHOTOS THAT LIRA CHUCKED AT me before stalking off. A son. I had a son. Even with all the tumultuous shit around me, a smile still crossed my face. I couldn't wait to see his face and watch him grow up. Thinking about *him* only made me think of *her* and how much it pained me to watch Lira leave. I hated being the reason why her beautiful face twisted into a knot, and the reason she walked out of my life fuming. Had she been a cartoon character, I was sure her head would've been ablaze. As much as it tormented me to do it, it had to be done. My icy relationship with Draya seemed to be thinning by the day, and I couldn't be the reason behind two broken hearts, even if I wanted Lira around. I walked upstairs to find Draya curled up in the fetal position on the bed, binge-watching episodes of Grey's Anatomy.

"It's done. Lira's gone," I announced, hoping that would put a smile on her face. When it didn't, I walked over to her and placed my hand on hers. "Did you hear what I said?"

"Yeah, mmhm."

"You're upset," I revealed, noticing the smug look on her face.

"I'm not."

"I know that face. That's your *I'm upset with Rome, but I ain't gon' say shit about it'* face. And your eyebrows - they get overly expressive when you're mad," I concluded, calling her bluff.

She pushed out a loud sigh. "I thought I would feel better with her gone, y'know? I thought her leaving was what I wanted, but it's not. I guess I still don't know what I want."

"Just give it time."

"How much time? I'm annoyed with being sad all the time."

"As much as it takes. Come on, let's go out tonight. Get dressed up, put on your sexiest dress, and let's go out. I wanna show you off tonight."

She flashed me a half-smile, which was something I hadn't seen her do in weeks. "Okay..."

Later that night, Draya and I pulled up to her favorite restaurant. As soon as we approached the hostess area, she turned to me with a smile.

"I'm so happy you had this idea, baby. I've missed things being just us."

"Yeah, me too."

"Do you think we'll be able to sit at my favorite table?"

"We can ask."

On our way to be seated, the hostess started to take us to the opposite side of the restaurant when Draya spoke up. "Actually, I was hoping we could be seated on the other side of the restaurant at my favorite table by the window," she stated.

"We can walk over and see if it's available," the hostess replied.

We followed behind the hostess to the other side of the restaurant. When we approached the table, Cash was sitting across from his date.

The moment her eyes landed on Cash, her smile seemed to disappear again, and the light went out of her eyes.

"What's up, bro?" I greeted him.

He reached out to dap me up. "Yo, what's up? I ain't think I was gon' run into y'all out here tonight. This is my date, Courtney."

"Nice to meet you; I'm Rome. This is my wife, Draya."

"Hi."

"Yeah, we ain't tryna crash your night; we were just trying to see if this table was available."

"It's my favorite," Draya interjected, shooting Cash a daggered look.

Cash's eyebrows rose to his forehead. "This is your favorite table? I had no idea."

"It's no problem, bro. We'll sit on the other side of the restaurant. Enjoy your night," I told him.

Cash nodded with a smile. "I'll hit you up tomorrow."

"Bet," I stated, dapping him up. "Let's go, bae."

I clung my arm around her waist as she snapped her neck back at him one last time before we walked off. After we ordered our drinks, I noticed all of Draya's attention had been swallowed up by her phone. With my glass in hand, I glanced over her shoulder to see Cash on his. The coincidence sparked a fire in me that was soon extinguished when I watched him put his away while she was still clicking.

I finished the last of my drink before I spoke. "You look beautiful tonight, even though you are mad about that table."

She looked up at me and forced a fake smile across her face before rolling her eyes. "Thank you, and I'll get over it, I guess."

"I got you something," I announced.

Her eyes googled with excitement from across the table. "A present? For me?"

"Yeah."

"What is it?"

I reached into my pocket, pulled out a velvet box, and slid it across the table. She opened it to see a platinum tennis bracelet laced with diamonds inside. She drew in a sharp breath with a smile before pulling it out of the box and handing it to me. I wrapped it around her soft skin and closed the clasp so she could admire it up close.

"You like it?" I inquired.

"I love it. Thank you so much, baby, for everything."

I was relieved my romantic gesture hadn't gone unnoticed. Draya's hot and cold mood swings had me feeling like things between us would never be the same again, but I made a promise the day I made her my wife. For better or for worse. I took that vow, and I had to stand by it. I would ride it out and do my best to push Lira to the back of my mind.

One week later.

Despite my efforts at keeping Lira at the back of my mind, she always managed to make her way back to the forefront. She ignored all my calls and texts since I told her she had to move out. I knew she was mad I'd switched up on her, but I couldn't not stand by my wife. I missed her presence. It wasn't until she left that I noticed how much of a void she left behind. What I didn't tell her about the apartment I set her up in was that I had private cameras installed throughout to be able to still look in on her whenever I wanted. I told myself it was for her safety when really, it was selfish. It was unhealthy. It was without consent. I acknowledged all that shit. Overall, it was my impulsive urge to be around her that prompted me to do anything in my power to keep her around, even from afar.

Secretly watching her only pissed me off more. She was growing by the day, and I missed the opportunity to see it unfold in person. Truthfully, I missed more than that. Even with all the darkness in her life, Lira had a unique light about her. It was something about her presence that was calming, nurturing even. A quality that Draya didn't have and one I couldn't buy her. I sat and watched Lira do her favorite thing, dance. It had quickly become my favorite thing to watch her do. I could sit and drool over the way her body moved with such grace and precision all day.

Suddenly, something inside me snapped, and I couldn't take the distance anymore. I grabbed my keys and headed out the front door. I tried talking myself out of showing up at her place unannounced and out of impulse up until I pulled into the complex parking lot. It was no use. My mind was made up. I locked my car and stalked up to her door to knock. One look at her face and the best kind of frustration coursed through me. I clenched my fists. I wanted to strangle her, kiss her, kill her, and lick every inch of her all at the same damn time.

LIRA

"Who wants that perfect love story anyway, anyway?
Cliche, cliche, cliche, cliche."

Beyonce's smooth, melodic voice bellowed through my Bluetooth speaker as I went over my choreographed routine for the fiftieth time, preparing for my studio elective final. I was excited about the dance routine I'd put together to Jay-Z and Beyonce's anthem *Part II (On the Run)*. Once I auditioned and got back into the program, I kept my head in the game to finish what I had started. Pregnant or not, there would be no more distractions. I was happy that some of my old professors were still there in the few years I'd been gone. Soon, I would be dancing in front of them and depending on them to give me the grade I needed to walk across the stage. I heard a knock on the door in the middle of my eight-count and didn't even flinch. Still in two minds, I paused the music and hurried to the door, ready to tell whoever was on the other side to go back where they came from. I swung the door open and froze. Rome stood on the other side of the door staring back at me.

"Am I interrupting you?" he asked.

"You kinda are," I informed him through my heavy breathing.

"What you in here doin'?"

"Dancing. I'm choreographing a routine for school."

"Word? Let me see what you put together," he insisted.

"Right now?"

"Yeah, right now. Why not?" he teased, attempting to step inside.

I held out my hand to stop him. "Um, who said I was gonna let you in? As far as I'm concerned, we still got beef."

He grabbed my hand and pressed it to his chest. "You can take that up with me *after* you dance for me."

I sucked my teeth. "Yeah, okay. Fine. You're gonna wanna back up, though," I advised, allowing him to come inside.

I restarted the song as Rome stood across the room with his eyes pinned on me. I stepped into the middle of the open living room floor. The wood creaked underneath my feet as I began to roll my neck and stretch.

I listened to her voice cascade through the speakers and gently started tapping my right foot while swaying my hips from side to side. I lifted my hands in the air while slowly twisting my wrists.

"Black hourglass, our glass,
   Toast to clichés in a dark past."

"One, two, three, four—five, six, seven, eight," I echoed, clicking my fingers as soon as the beat dropped.

The rhythm pulsed through me as I slowly popped my ass while running my hands down the front of my body and over my curves. I slow rocked to the beat while gliding my hands up my tapered leg. Being pregnant, I was limited to arc-like leg gestures instead of the soaring leaps and complex movements I was used to in my choreographed routines. My pointed feet slid in and out of closed positions as I gracefully spun like a top around the room, taking up as much square footage as possible, showcasing my strength and personal style.

"And if loving you is a crime,
Tell me why do I bring out the best in you."

As the song went on, I felt more in my element, sinking deeper into my perfectly coordinated dance combination. My routine was sensual, filled with wide steps and twisting hips that could wind, pop, dip, and snap. The lyrics moved across the beat as my arms and legs tore through the air, hair whipping in every direction across my face. The dance faculty required excellence, and I was prepared to give it to them. Rome's eyes outlined my every move as I correctly aligned my spine before I rose my arm and supported my body on one leg while the other was extended straight behind me. Our gaze remained locked as I danced; one rhythmic and dynamic move after the other. I took my body to the ground, curling my tailbone before stretching all of my limbs as gracefully as an angel.

"And if loving you had a price,
I would pay my life for you."

The song ended, and I stood waiting for his applause to die down. My heart thumped as I made my way over to him.

"So, what do you think?" I questioned.

"That shit was fire."

"Thanks. I'm still tweaking a few things. My final is coming up soon, so I have to finalize it in the next few days."

"I think it's perfect. It was sexy but graceful, and at the same time, you could still feel the gutta in it."

I smiled. "I'm glad it struck a chord with you."

"It did. I couldn't take my eyes off you. What was your inspiration behind it?"

"You," I confessed. He was my silent muse and had been for months.

His lips curled with anger. "Why the fuck you playin' with me, Lira?"

I shrugged. "You asked."

He shot me a look that told me he was unraveling more and more by the second. "So, once you do this, you're officially done with school?"

I proudly bobbed my head. "Yup. Graduation is so close I can taste it, only a few months away."

"Word? I'm so fuckin' proud of you. I can't wait to see you walk across the stage."

My eyes lit up in surprise. "You'd come? Don't feel obligated to–"

"Of course, I'd come. I ain't never go to college or nothin' like that, but I know that shit isn't easy. And for that, you deserve to be celebrated."

His words brought a grin to my lips. "Well, thank you..."

"I'm amazed at how fluid your body moves, even with you being pregnant. You look beautiful," he complimented me.

My eyes slid down to the floor. "Stop that."

"What?"

"Stop talking to me like that."

"I can't help myself. I created life inside you. That's nothin' I take lightly."

"Six months today," I announced," I feel good, though."

"Time is flying. Soon, lil' man will be running around the house."

"About that, I shouldn't have–"

"Nah, you ain't gotta apologize. I know I blindsided you with that shit, but I didn't come here to talk about that."

"What did you come here to talk about then?" I quizzed.

"I wanted to check on you, make sure you've got everything you need here since you been ignorin' me and shit."

I nodded; eyes torn wide. "I'm fine, Rome. You know I'm fine."

We stared each other down, submerging in the silence. The way he looked at me made me feel like I was standing in front of him wearing nothing. Unable to take the quiet, I spoke up. "Rome, you–"

"I came here because I can't stay the fuck away from you if I tried," he admitted.

Rome reached out and tucked a loose strand of my hair behind my ear, and I felt my knees buckle. I was pathetic. Pregnant, pathetic, and horny as hell. It had been months since I'd been touched. I'd spent so much time with my vibrator that I'd forgotten what human contact felt like.

"You should probably, uh…you know, go…before."

"Before what? You wanted to know why I came here, right?"

"You should go," I stated, dropping one foot back.

He stepped closer. "What if I don't wanna go? Because the way I'm feelin' right now, you might have to kick my ass out."

My heart thudded seconds before he grabbed my face and let his lips take possession of mine. After many long and relentless seconds, I slowly pulled away.

"We can't," I disagreed, teeth sinking into my bottom lip, "we agreed."

He gripped my ass, crashing our bodies even closer together. "Stop biting that fuckin' lip," he growled, "that's my job."

Rome kissed me again, sinking his teeth into my lip before gently sucking on it.

The warmth between our bodies grew hotter by the second. His hands skated down my curves and then caressed my stomach. I gripped his muscular biceps as he lightly pressed my back against the wall. He buried his soft lips into my neck, pressing tender kisses there too.

"Are you gonna kick me out?" he mumbled; lips still mashed against my skin.

"Not a chance."

"Good." He maintained a smile before scooping me into his arms and carrying me down the hallway to my bedroom. He gently laid me across my unmade bed and slid off my leggings and sports bra before caressing my breasts. I felt my nipples getting hard as diamonds in his hands. The loud sound of my thudding heartbeat was enough to drive me crazy. All my body wanted to focus on was the moment, but my mind was racing as if I was losing my virginity. As much as I wanted him to pleasure me from top to bottom, a part of me still had my reservations.

"You ever been with a pregnant woman before?" I asked, partly joking, partly serious.

Rome snickered. "Nah, you'd be my first."

"I'm nervous," I admitted.

"Don't be. I'ma take good care of you."

"I haven't...been with, y'know, anyone since we last...."

He nodded before snatching his shirt over his head. "I got you. All of you," he assured me.

Rome licked up my neck as my fingertips drifted across his tattoo-inked skin. His fingers dug into my hips, hastily tugging my panties to the side before disappearing between my brown thighs. I was so caught up in the moment that I neglected the shower I knew my body needed after rehearsing. I tossed my head back, mesmerized by how his tongue made love to my tender flesh.

"I wanna shower. Let me shower," I declared.

"I don't care."

"Please," I whined.

"I want you now," he confessed, flicking his tongue against my clit.

I spread my legs from east to west and pointed my feet downward. He snaked his tongue up and down my sex, causing my toes to curl under. I looked down at him, hypnotized by the tongue lashing he gave me. He slurped and sucked against my clit before inching two

.L. Hall

fingers inside me. His warm brown orbs flashed up to meet mine as his fingers twisted and thrust inside my ocean.

Rome smirked as the chain around his neck brushed against my skin. "That pussy gushin'."

The rest of his clothes came off, and he walked into the bathroom to turn on the shower. After letting it heat up, he returned to me and finished undressing me. We got inside the shower together, and he washed my body from head to toe. After rinsing the soap off my back, he slid the tip of his dick up and down against my slit from behind. I slowly rocked back against him, taking every inch. He spread my pussy lips, letting the water droplets bounce off my clit. He bent me forward, kissing down my spine as I extended my arms against the marble shower wall. I sucked in air through my teeth as his thickness pulsed inside me. He pressed his palm into my lower back.

"R–Rome," I breathed.

"Fuck, you're soaking for me," he whispered against my neck.

"It feels so good," I proclaimed, keeping my back arched as Rome entangled his arms around my waist. I grabbed his wrists and slowly rocked back against him, creaming all over him.

"That's it, baby girl. Cum on daddy's dick. Make a mess with that pussy."

He pulled my hair back and drew my lips to his before sliding his thumb inside my asshole.

"Mmmm, fuck!" I screamed, bouncing up and down on him as he pumped one deep stroke after the other.

His lips found my neck as he cupped my breasts in his hands. His fingertips toyed with my nipples as I gyrated my hips.

"Ah shit, this pussy is too good. I wanna taste it again. Can I taste it again?" he mumbled against the nape of my neck.

Before I could respond, he eased out of me and dropped to his knees. His teeth sunk into the dimple in my ass before inching down to eat my ass and pussy from behind. I arched my back, gluing my fingertips to the shower tile as if I was Spiderman.

Rome jiggled my ass between his lips before licking up and down my crack.

"Oooh shit. Just like that," I purred, looking back at him.

"You like that shit?"

"Mmhm."

Rome caressed my ass while he feasted on my flesh some more before we got out and dried off to continue in the bedroom. He propped pillows all around me to ensure I was comfortable. Rome laid behind me and tossed my legs over to the side before easing back inside me. My fingertips grazed across the sheets as he dipped in and out of my sweet spot. Feeling every inch, I sunk my unmanicured nails into his thighs while twisting my hips against him.

"Keep fuckin' me just like that. Gimme every drop of that pussy," Rome growled in my ear as I continued to bounce back against him.

Two rounds of mind-blowing sex later, I was lying in Rome's arms while he caressed my bare stomach. If I never got a chance to experience what absolute heaven was like, being there with him was as close as I'd ever get.

"Why do you always do that?" Rome asked, glancing down at me.

I tilted my head upward. "Do what?"

"Smile like you're about to cry."

"Maybe because I ain't ever had nothin' to smile about that didn't end with me in tears," I confessed, refusing to be anything but raw at the moment.

"What I tell you about that? You're good with me."

I shook my head, not wanting to deal with my feelings. Dealing with them meant snapping out of my euphoric delirium. I was happily caught up in the rapture of his stroke. I missed it, and I wasn't ready to leave it. "Why are you worried about me? Why don't you tell me what's going on in your head right now," I nudged.

"Right now?" he asked.

"Yeah, right now."

He turned to look at me as if he could see right through to my soul. "I think I gotta leave my wife."

CASH

IT HAD BEEN A COUPLE OF WEEKS SINCE SEEING DRAYA OUT WITH ROME while I was with Courtney. I knew damn well that was Draya's favorite table, but having the opportunity to see the look on her face when I pretended I didn't realize was too priceless to pass up. Truthfully, I only started seeing Courtney to piss her off. She was nice, but we both knew she was a placeholder until Draya decided to come to her senses. My mind flashed back to our text conversation that night in the restaurant. I'd been icing her out ever since.

DRAY:

My favorite table, though? Real classy.

ME:

You jealous?

DRAY:

I'm not jealous.

137

ME:

Okay. Enjoy your night.

DRAY:

When were you planning to tell me about your
date? She's cute, but she ain't me.

ME:

I told you how I felt about you, and you dipped.
Now you see me out, and now you in your
feelings? I'm done waiting for you. I've moved
on. Don't hit my phone anymore.

My phone vibrated, prompting me to zone back into the present and look at the screen. I answered for Rome. "What's up?"

"You busy? I want you to ride out with me."

"Where to?"

"Just out."

My eyebrow arched. "Everything good?"

"Yeah."

"Aight. Um, I'm at the crib right now if you wanna slide through."

"Cool. I'll pick you up in fifteen," he replied before ending the call.

While waiting for Rome to arrive, I scrolled through my Instagram feed when I came across a picture Draya recently posted of her and Rome. The caption read, *'If it's me and you against the world, then so be it.'* I scoffed. Their relationship was a fuckin' joke, and we both knew it. She was posting about my best friend like they had a picture-perfect relationship when secretly, she was on my line trying to get me to talk to her. All I ever got from Draya was one mixed signal after the other. I debated texting her back for a second, but when Rome arrived, I let the thought fade and went outside to ride out with my boy.

"What's been going on? Everything better since Lira moved out?" I asked, starting off the conversation as Rome drove.

"If you describe quiet as better, then I guess."

"What do you mean?"

"Dray, she's still...not herself."

"What's wrong with her?"

"She's been going through some personal shit, and she wanted some space, so that's why I had Lira move out in the first place. But shit still ain't better."

"Do you miss her?"

"Who? Lira?"

I dipped my head in a quick nod. "Yeah."

He glanced over at me before sliding his eyes back to the road. His look alone didn't require words for me to know he did. I nodded to let him know I understood. Inside, I was tired of being a sounding board to my best friend about his love triangle when he still didn't know about mine. I debated spilling everything to him about my relationship with Draya to make it easier for him to choose between Draya and Lira. The words were right on the tip of my tongue, but I couldn't do it. Not because I didn't want to, but because I knew Draya would hate me if I did. Instead, I decided to give him a piece of advice that would hopefully sway him in the arms of Lira. If Draya wasn't going to leave him, maybe I could persuade Rome to leave her. I was willing to do anything to make Draya come crawling back to me and stay.

"You can go back and forth about something in your mind a million times, but it all comes down to what your heart says at the end of the day."

He tweaked his lips to the side. "All of a sudden, you goin' soft on me?"

I let out a soft chuckle. "Nah. I could tell you what you want to hear. I could tell you what I think you should do. I just know that none of it will matter when it comes down to it."

He sighed. "I don't know what the fuck I'ma do."

"The right decision will reveal itself to you when the time comes," I assured him.

Later that night, after getting home from being out with Rome, Draya showed up at my place. I guess she was tired of me avoiding coming by her house and dodging her texts and calls, so she figured she'd corner me at my house.

"You're bold."

"So I've been told," she responded, arms folded tight across her chest.

"Rome know you here?"

"Don't worry about all that. Can we talk?"

"I can't. I got company," I disclosed, although I was alone.

She sucked her teeth. "Tell that bitch to go home. I have to talk to you. It's important."

"About what?"

"You know what, Cash. Stop playing with me. I've been having a hard time lately, and you ignoring me isn't helping."

I sucked my teeth before opening the door more and sliding out of the way so that she could come inside.

"I thought you said you had company."

"I thought you said you wanted to talk," I retorted.

Air hissed through a crack in her tight, glossy lips. "Fine. You still seein' Courtney?"

"What if I am?"

"Is she a better lover than me?"

My lips narrowed. "What?"

"Are you in love with her like you're in love with me?"

"Draya, what the fuck is wrong with you? You have been blowin' up my phone for weeks, and now you're here in my face, and the first thing you wanna know is if I'm fuckin' her? What's next? You wanna know if my dick makes her cum as many times as it makes you cum?"

"Cash, I–"

"Do you ever mean the shit you say, or only when I'm fuckin' you?

Because when I'm fuckin' you, I can call you baby. When I'm fuckin' you, it's mine and only mine, and it's the best dick you've ever had. You're full of shit; you know that? You made it clear where we stood, so I moved on."

"What's clear is that you wanted to hurt me, so you did."

"So, seeing me with another bitch is what it takes to get some emotion out of you?"

"I guess so."

"Say it."

She snapped her eyes at me. "Say what?"

"Say it hurt you to see me out with someone else. I wanna hear you say the words, Dray."

Air left her nostrils in a rush. "Look, I know I made a mistake! You don't need to rub it in!"

"Say it!" I roared.

Her eyes glowered with tears. "I don't want to talk about it anymore. I don't even know why I came here," she hissed, heading for the door.

I watched her walk away. "There you go running away because you think that's what everyone expects you to do. But I know you, Dray. You're not as empty as you lead others to believe."

She turned back to me with eyes so hazy that she could barely see a foot in front of her. I hurried to her, and she crumpled like a rag doll in my arms. She started crying hysterically. "I can't just ... you can't expect me to give you the answers you wanna hear. I'm trying my best! Doesn't that count for something?"

"How much longer are we gonna do this dance? Huh, Dray?" I asked, firmly shaking her shoulders.

"I'm not ready, Cash. I don't know if I'll ever be."

"Then, why the fuck are you here?" I flared.

"I was pregnant, okay? I was pregnant, and I lost the baby!" she confessed.

141

DRAYA

I'D SAID THE WORDS I TOLD MYSELF I'D NEVER TELL HIM. IT WAS OUT IN the open. After losing the baby, I'd been going through one rollercoaster ride of emotions. Seeing Cash out with another woman didn't do anything but fuel my sadness. A part of me felt like he deserved to know about the baby possibly being his. The other wanted a reason to see him. A reason for him to touch me, cater to me, anything to siphon out the pain.

"Was it mine?" he asked.

"Excuse me?"

"I've been fucking you for months; I have the right to know."

I exhaled a quick breath. "Truthfully, I—I don't know."

"So, I'm supposed to be okay that you were possibly carrying my child? The seed that I put inside you? And you didn't even bother to tell me until now? You figured you'd sweep it under the rug and I wouldn't question it?"

"What does it even matter now? It's dead! I lost it!"

"That's not the point, and you know it!"

"You know what? I made a mistake coming here."

"You can't keep pretending it didn't happen, 'cause guess what? It did!"

I shook my head. "I knew I never should've said anything. If I would've known you'd be all in your feelings, I wouldn't have."

"Draya, don't go," he pleaded, reaching for my arm. "I didn't mean to upset you more than you already are. If I had known the moment it happened, I would've been there for you. I never wanna see you hurt if I can help it."

He pulled my body back into his, and I sobbed into his shirt. "I'm so sorry I lost our baby, Cash."

He stroked my hair and held me tight, giving me the TLC I'd been craving. "Shh. Shh. It's okay, baby. It's okay."

"There you go again with the baby shit!" I challenged, pushing him away.

I knew I was being hot and cold with him, but emotionally I was all over the place, and I couldn't help myself.

"Dray, I'm just trying to be there for you the best way I know how."

"Why? Because I finally shed a tear on your shoulder? I'm fine, Cash!"

"Are you trying to start an argument right now?"

"No, I'm trying to end this," I breathed. "I should've stopped fucking you the moment you told me you loved me, and I didn't."

"And why didn't you, Dray? Why didn't you stop? Because you love me! Why can't you say it?"

"Because saying it fixes nothing! It changes nothing! How many times do I have to tell you that!" I screamed.

Cash crinkled up his nose in disgust before shaking his head. His next move surprised me. I watched him walk over to the front door and open it for me. "I can't keep doing this with you, Dray. You have to choose. It's Rome or me."

"Loving me is a death sentence, Cash. We both know that," I chided before walking out the door.

I got back inside my car, realizing that Cash was too fragile for me to put all my trust in. I had to figure out my next move, and it had to be something that didn't involve me having to rely on him. I repeatedly tapped my fingers against the steering wheel as the gears inside my head turned all the way home. Although Lira was no longer underneath my roof, Rome may have had more feelings for her than he'd led me to believe. I was desperate for an insurance policy to ensure my marriage stayed intact. We were already on shaky ground, and I refused to let it crumble underneath me.

After tossing and turning all night, I woke up the following day and crept into a quiet corner of the house. With the phone pressed to my ear, I called in an anonymous tip to the police station to report Lira's boyfriend as missing and plant the seed that he may have been murdered. My intention wasn't to get my husband caught up, but if I could somehow get Rome to find out that the police were sniffing around Lira, I could get him to see she was nothing but the disloyal thief she was when her feet first touched the pavement of our driveway.

LIRA

I TREKKED DOWN THE CAMPUS WALKWAY LINED WITH PALM TREES THAT stretched to the clouds with my dance bag slung over my shoulder. As happy as I was to have been accepted back into the dance program, the coursework was no joke. Between in-class rehearsals in my Dance Senior Seminar, rehearsing for my upcoming showcase, and the pregnancy, being a full-time college student was kicking my ass. Not to mention, all dance majors were required to always maintain a grade point average of 3.0. USF's dance program was highly selective. If it hadn't been for some of the same dance faculty still being there and agreeing to be my references, I probably wouldn't have had a fighting chance. Although I'd been of school for a few years, I never stopped practicing. I continued to dance any chance I got to keep my skills tight for the day I would return.

I headed to my car while replaying the last eight-count I'd finished rehearsing in my head. I was so lost in thought that I slammed right into someone's shoulder as they passed by.

"Oh shit, excuse me!" I emphasized, gathering myself.

"No problem. I'm actually looking for the bookstore. Can you tell me if I'm headed in the right direction? This is a pretty big campus," he remarked, flashing me a warm smile.

I rendered a light laugh before giving him a once-over. He was dressed in a plain black hoodie and matching joggers with neon Nike sneakers on his feet. His sleeves were rolled up to his forearms, showcasing the tattoos carved across his sandy brown skin.

"Yeah, you're a little lost. What you're gonna wanna do is head to the opposite side of campus, past the student center and USF Bull Market. Once you get on Cedar Drive, you can't miss it," I instructed.

"Thank you..." he paused, fishing for my name.

"Lira," I replied.

"Thanks, Lira. I'm Miguel Martinez. Agent Miguel Martinez," he said, quickly flashing me his badge.

The smile I'd worn instantly vanished. My heart sunk to my feet and a scowl scribbled across my face. "What? Why the fuck would you pretend to be lost? You're a creep. Stay the fuck away from me!"

"I need to speak with you about your boyfriend, Jevan!" he called out.

I snapped my neck in his direction, ready to clarify what I'd heard. "My what?"

"Your boyfriend."

"I don't have a boyfriend. I have to go," I said, walking in the opposite direction.

He jogged to my side. "We still haven't found his body. All I need you to do is tell me what you know."

I waved him off. "I don't know shit."

"We got a call. Someone reported him missing. I went around and talked to his boys, and they said the last person they saw him with before he disappeared was you, and that was months ago."

"Actually, we broke up months ago. He went his way, and I went mine. I don't have anything to do with him."

"You and I both know that's not true."

I halted my stride to face him. "Let me make something very clear to you, okay? Whatever you wanna know, I don't have the answers to. So just, leave me alone!"

"I know he was murdered, Lira, and I think you either did it, or know who did."

I narrowed a frown at him. "Like I said, I don't have the answers you're looking for."

He reached inside his pocket and pulled out his business card. "Hold onto this if you change your mind."

"No need, because I won't," I informed him.

His hand extended to mine, flipping it open to place the card in my palm. "You might. I'll be in touch. Oh, and congratulations on the baby," he said, eyeing my stomach.

Agent Martinez stalked off in the opposite direction, leaving me standing in the middle of the paved walkway. I shook my head, trying to calm my nerves, and shoved the card inside my bag. I'd seen my share of police throughout the years for petty crimes nonetheless; so often, I knew when to call bullshit. I didn't know why Agent Martinez was sniffing around me, nor did I know why he had Jevan's name in his mouth. He'd been dead for months, and I hadn't heard a peep about a missing person's or anything. I needed to be prepared with a story about what happened between us to throw him off my trail so that I wouldn't inevitably lead him to Rome.

ROME

One week later.

Now that Lira and I seemed to be back on good terms, I decided to stop by the apartment and drop in with some food. I had no intention of staying long, but my devotion to her nutrition while she was carrying my son gave me a reason to see her glow in person. I swiped the tied-plastic bag of food from the passenger seat and headed across the parking lot when I caught a glimpse of Agent Martinez right before he dipped his head inside his car.

"What the fuck?" I mumbled.

I quickened my stride to Lira's door and banged without regard to her neighbors. As soon as Lira opened the door, I spoke. "Did you have company?"

Her eyes bugged, then went back to their standard size. "What? No."

"You sure?" I asked.

She let out a sharp exhale. "You're the one who popped up here out of nowhere. Just ask me what you wanna ask me, Rome."

"Why the fuck was that fuckin' fed here, and what did he want?"

A robust breath left her lungs. "Look, I was gonna tell you, alright? I was just trying to make it go away on my own."

"Make what go away?"

"He–he wanted to talk about Jevan. He said he knows he's dead, and he thinks I did it or that I know who did."

Her words lit a fire in the pit of my stomach. "And how would he know anything about that nigga unless you said something?"

"I didn't say anything to him!"

"Then, why the fuck was he in this apartment?" I hollered, crunching the bag with my fists.

I'd forgotten all about her food the moment I saw that snake. "I swear I didn't let him past the door! He was only here for a few minutes if that. He said what he said about Jevan, and I told him that I didn't know anything. He asked me why I hadn't given him a call and left me another one of his stupid business cards."

Shock unhitched my jaw. "Hold up. *Another one?*"

"I ran into him about a week ago. He pulled up on me at school and tried to intimidate me. I didn't say shit, and he gave me his card. That's all."

I walked into the kitchen and tossed the food I'd brought on the counter. "Anything else you wanna get off your fuckin' chest?" I griped.

There was a momentary pause as Lira's eyes linked with mine. "Actually, there is something else I need to tell you."

My eyes sliced into hers, studying the look of anguish on her face. "What else?"

Her chest rose and fell before she took her seat. "You remember when you asked me what I knew about Jevan and his family?"

"Yeah."

"Well, I left out some things that I think you should know."

"What things?"

"He said that robbing your spot was only the beginning and that you and your brothers haven't seen anything yet. When his brother gets out of jail, something is going to go down."

I levied a glare at her. "Something like what?"

"He didn't say."

"Did he say when Bankx was gettin' out?"

"In another year or so, but I don't know how true that is. He could've just been talking shit. But whenever it is, he said Miami better take cover, and in the streets, it's a life for a life."

"Why the fuck are you telling me this shit now?" I barked.

"He called me his family, y'know? I told you I've never had that, ever. I wanted to trust him, and you took him from me! Why would I tell you something like that right away? Jevan's been a ghost to me for months, and it's like he's coming back from the dead without warning, and I–I'm not a liar. M–maybe I'm not always one hundred percent honest, and I know the timing is bad. It might even look like I'm trying to save my ass right now, and maybe a part of me is, y'know? Because at first, I planned to keep it in my back pocket and use it as leverage. Then the baby happened, and then I was living under your roof. It never seemed like the right time to say anything," she confessed as tears swept down her cheeks.

Her tears didn't affect me the least bit. "Not saying anything is just as bad as lying."

"I'm sorry. It was a mistake, okay? I made a mistake by not telling you, but what has changed now that you know? Nothing! He's still in jail, and Jevan is still dead!"

"Are you fuckin' kidding me? This changes everything!"

"Can't you see I'm trying to make things right?"

"Ain't shit right between us right now, Lira," I declared. "Draya was right. You're not who I thought you were."

Lira's brows sloped. "What does *she* have to do with any of this?"

"Everything. She's my wife!"

She scoffed. "Only when it's convenient for you!"

I brushed her off. "Yeah, whatever."

"Why don't you just admit it?"

"Admit what?" I grumbled.

"That you want me out of your life so bad that you look for any little reason to dismiss me, but it makes you sick to your stomach to even think about letting me leave. That's why you got me here! Tucked away in a fuckin' corner like a plaything! I can't believe I agreed to have a baby by your ass! I swear to God, I can't wait to drop this baby and be done with you! With all of this!" she roared.

Both of our emotions were on ten. It didn't matter if she was right. It didn't matter if I was wrong. Nothing mattered but the fact that she lied. "Fuck you, Lira," I spat before darting toward the front door.

She raced after me. "Fuck me, Rome? That's all you have to say to me?" When I didn't respond, she spoke up again. "I'm sorry! I don't know how many times you want me to say it! I'm sorry! Please don't leave me! Please don't go! I don't want to be alone, Rome, please!" she screamed, hysterically clawing at my shirt.

I pushed her off. "Get the fuck off me!"

"Rome!"

"Get your fuckin' hands off me, Lira!"

"Please stay. I'm sorry! I'm sorry, Rome! This is the most painful mistake I've ever made in my life, and I see that now! I see it! Please stay!" she pleaded.

"You think I wanna leave? I never wanna leave you!" I admitted.

Lira had a face I didn't want to lie to. A face I *couldn't* lie to. Things had been up and down like a tidal wave since we met.

"Then don't. Please don't give up on me. You're all I have, Rome," she admitted, pressing her head against my chest.

I'd never been scared to say how I felt, but I knew the words that were about to slip off my tongue would hurt like hell.

"Maybe you were right when you said none of this was real. Because you're a dream to me, Lira, only a fool would have to think twice about lovin' you. And I do, Lira. I do love you, but I can't."

"Why not?"

I pried her arms from around my waist. "Because I don't trust you! I don't trust you, and I promised to stay with my wife. I'ma stand on my word, no matter how hard it is for me to quit you."

"Rome, please don't say it!"

151

"I'm done with you, Lira. Whatever this shit is between us is done. The moment you have my son, you'll get your wish, and you'll be done with me and with everything. Draya and I will raise him as our own like we agreed, and it'll be like everything between us never happened," I promised.

I slammed the door behind me, leaving her screaming hysterically on the other side. Frustrated, I got back in my car and pulled out my phone to text Draya.

ME:

Dinner tonight?

DRAYA:

I'll make reservations at our favorite spot.

ME:

Bet.

DRAYA:

Can't wait. I'm glad we're getting back to us, baby.

ME:

Yeah, me too.

CASH

IT WAS TWO O'CLOCK IN THE MORNING, AND MY PHONE BUZZED WITH yet another mixed signal from Draya. She was the queen of sending mixed fuckin' signals, and it was driving me insane.

DRAY:

You up?

ME:

Where's your man?

DRAY:

Asleep. I'm texting you from the bathroom.

ME:

Why?

DRAY:

...

153

The three ellipses appeared, disappeared, and then reappeared again. Impatient and frustrated, I tossed the phone beside me and rolled over to light my blunt. I hated waiting until that nigga was in Lala Land before hearing from her. I tossed and turned all night, debating whether to show up at Rome's house and confront them both. I was sick and tired of her playing games with both of us. I had opportunity after opportunity to blow up her whole spot, and I never did because I was trying to be respectful of what she wanted and give her time to figure out that I was the man she needed to be with. I was tired of being an afterthought and constantly having to put my feelings on the backburner. For the first time, I would fight for what I wanted.

By six o'clock that morning, I found myself taking a cold shower after doing three long lines of coke. Forty-five minutes later, I found myself parked in Rome's driveway with no clear recollection of my arrival. The drugs I took had me wired as fuck. I stumbled out of my car and up to his front door. My knuckles delivered a sluggish knock before I repeatedly laid my finger against the doorbell, hoping to wake up the entire house. Rome swung the door open a few minutes later with a frown. It softened when he saw me, and then he yawned.

"I know I shouldn't be here," I started.

"What's wrong with you, Cash? You aight, nigga? You look crazy."

"I ain't crazy!" I hissed.

His brow lifted in concern. "I'm worried about you. You sure you aight?"

"Don't be. I'm good."

"You sure?"

"I said I'm good!" I barked.

"What the fuck is wrong with you then? It's not even eight o'clock."

"You gon' let me in or not?"

He silently eyed me from the top of my head to my feet. "I'm not stepping aside until you back up, nigga."

"Really? That's how you gon' do me? But you know what, I deserve that shit. I do."

"What are you talkin' about?"

"I was your friend, and I fucked up. This is on me."

Rome's face turned cold. "What happened? What did you do, Cash?" he asked, pulling me inside.

"I'm in love," I confessed.

He pushed out two notes of a chuckle. "In love? Nigga, with who?"

"With Dray."

His coy smile vanished, and his demeanor returned to stone-cold. "What the fuck did you just say to me?"

"I'm in love with Dray," I repeated.

"What the fuck do you mean you're in love with Dray? She's my wife!"

"I ain't want you to find out like this, bro, but I'm tired of lying and hiding. You deserve to know the truth."

"And the truth is what? That my best friend has been fuckin' my wife behind my back?"

"I know it hurts to hear, but–"

"Were you fuckin' her before I married her?"

"No."

"So, you waited until she became my wife to–yeah, aight. Get the fuck out of my house before I beat the shit out of you!"

"I'm not leaving without her," I stated.

His forehead became a maze of wrinkles, and his brows plunged. "You gon' be leavin' in a body bag if you don't step. You ain't welcome in my shit or anywhere else around me ever again. You see me walkin' down the street, you move your ass to the other fuckin' side, aight? That's the shit I'm on from here on out!" his voice boomed.

"I'm not leaving here without her," I repeated, standing my ground.

Rome ripped out a laugh in my face. "The wildest part about all of this shit is you couldn't even be a dog and keep it pushin'. You had to fuck around and fall in love with her, but guess what? Dray's mine, aight? She's mine!"

I shook my head while swiping my dreads away from my face. "As always, Rome gotta have is cake and another cake, too. You a selfish ass nigga, you know that? You got a wife, yet you got another bitch carryin' your seed. Everybody knows you're in love with Lira except you! But can't nobody else be happy unless Rome is happy, huh?"

I kept quiet about many of Rome's moves in his personal life, but his ass needed to be checked. Usually, it wasn't my business, but Draya was my business, and he'd hurt her. No matter if she wanted to admit it, I knew Rome broke her heart when he told her he wanted Lira to keep the baby. Draya neglected her needs for Rome, and I'd neglected mine for hers. The cycle needed to end.

He chuckled in my face, rocking with silent laughter as if everything I told him was a comedic act. "So, all the times I asked you about Draya, you told me you ain't find shit out, and she wasn't out here doin' shit on the side, all of it was a lie? I was trying to watch out for her when I should've been watching out for you the entire time. Nigga, I ought to beat the fuck out of you!" Rome threatened.

I widened my stance out of instinct, ready to tussle if it came down to it.

"What the hell is going on with all this yelling?" Draya asked, hitting the bottom step wearing a silk bathrobe.

Rome snapped his neck toward her. "Is there somethin' you wanna fuckin' tell me?"

"You ain't gotta say shit to him that I ain't already said, Dray. Get your shit, bae. Let's go," I told her.

She looked at me with eyes doubled in size and a pouty lip. "What? Cash, what are you talking about? Are–are you okay?"

"I'm fine. You know I'm fuckin' fine!"

Her eyes remained alert as she tightened her satin robe around her waist. "Cash, don't do this here, okay? You should go home and sleep off whatever you have in your system," she advised.

"Both of you are gon' stop fuckin' talkin' to me like I'm fuckin' crazy, aight?"

"This mothafucka says y'all in love," Rome interjected, "is it true?"

"Rome, I–"

"Is it fuckin' true?" he cursed.

The three of us stood in silence, letting our eyes say things our lips wouldn't. Rome took a step back and looked at us with a crazed look. "You know what, it don't even fuckin' matter. Both of y'all asses got three seconds to leave my fuckin' property before I get my fuckin' gun. Whoever is standin' here where I get back is gon' get they head blown smooth off their shoulders," he warned.

"Let's go, Dray!" I instructed.

Instead of coming to my side, Draya turned her back to me and chased after Rome without a second thought. "No, Rome. Please!" Draya sobbed, reaching out to stop him from getting to his nearest weapon.

"Bitch, don't touch me!" he hollered, knocking her back a few steps.

"Draya, let's go!"

"No!"

"You heard that mothafucka; go with him!" Rome demanded.

"Rome, please! Let me tell you everything, and we can talk about it! You haven't even heard my side yet!"

"You think I give a fuck about anything you have to say? Get the fuck out of my sight, bitch," he grumbled.

I cuffed Draya's wrist and yanked her toward the door. "Let's go, Dray! It's over! Rome doesn't want you anymore! Can't you see that?"

"Can I at least put on some clothes and leave my house with some fuckin' dignity?" she pleaded, eyes swollen and red.

Rome cut his red-rimmed eyes at Draya. "Put your fuckin' clothes on, and then both of y'all get the fuck out. Ain't bout to be no more talkin' in a few more seconds," Rome threatened again before stalking off.

He came back a few minutes later, darting past me to run up the stairs to hurry Draya along. "Did I say pack a fuckin' bag, Dray? Throw on a shirt and get the fuck out!" he barked.

I ran up the stairs to her rescue to see Rome standing off to the side with a gun pointed right at Draya. "Rome, just let her get her shit, and then we leavin'!" I fumed, instantly regretting leaving my gun tucked underneath my seat. I prayed we both made it out of there alive.

DRAYA

My mouth hung to the ground as Cash ushered me out of my house like a stranger and into his car. He hurried around to the driver's seat and started the engine. Before I knew it, we were on the interstate. I sat straight up in my seat and twisted my neck in Cash's direction. Rage boiled inside me.

"Why the fuck would you do that? You ruined everything! He will never forgive either one of us!" I screamed.

"That nigga don't love you, Dray! Don't you get that? He's in love with Lira, and you know it!"

"Shut up! Just shut up!"

"Why won't you let me take care of you? Huh? All I've ever done is fuckin' love you, Dray. And your ass ain't never been satisfied."

"It doesn't matter what you'd do for me or how much you love me. You'll never be Rome!"

"And you'll never be Lira."

I cut my rage-filled eyes at him as tears streamed out ot my face. My words were caught in my throat, and I was choking on them. As much as I hated to admit it, he was right. It was one thing to fuck another woman, but to give his heart away was something I couldn't take. Against all logic, I smacked my full lips before letting the first thing on my mind fly out.

"I want that bitch dead!"

Cash darted his eyes away from the road to look at me. "You serious?"

My chest hitched as I tried to speak. "Yeah."

"I know where she stays," he replied while reaching underneath his seat. He pulled out a gun, laid it in my lap, and continued, "If you really 'bout that shit."

My eyes widened as I looked down at my lap. Now with a destination in mind, Cash mashed his foot on the gas, causing me to grip the side of the door. I looked over at him. The wind whipped his dreads across his face as he bobbed and weaved through traffic with no seatbelt on. It was the first time I'd looked at him all day, and I noticed white residue underneath his nose.

"Cash, are you high?" I asked.

He snapped his neck toward me. "What?"

"Are you high?"

"Who gives a fuck if I am? Shit, I got some more on me if you about that shit, too. We gon' have a good time, baby. Trust me; I got you."

He reached into his center console and pulled out a small, clear plastic bag with white powder inside. I watched in surprise as he popped the bag open, scooped some powder under his pinky nail, and shoved it up his nostrils. He sniffed hard and tossed his head back. Cash's eyes were rolled halfway to the back of his skull and not focused on the road.

"Watch the fuckin' road!" I screamed, snapping his high ass back into the present.

"My fault, baby. Don't worry, I'm good! Here, it's your turn!"

I stared at the bag in silence for a few seconds, unsure of what to do. If I took it, he'd expect me to do it. And if I didn't, he was so high out of his mind, I didn't know what he would do. I transferred the coke from his hand to mine and swept the tiniest amount possible inside my left nostril. Seconds later, I was feeling lightheaded and dizzy. Cash continued to speed to the apartment complex Lira lived in, which surprisingly wasn't too far from my home, which had Rome written all over it. We got out of the car and headed to Lira's apartment to kill the bitch that stole my husband.

I STEPPED OUT OF THE SHOWER AND WRAPPED THE OVERSIZED, PLUSH towel around my body when I heard a loud bang. I instinctively muted my ninety's R&B playlist to see if I heard the noise again and determine where it came from. A few seconds later, the loud thump happened again and again. I peeked my head out of the room and slowly crept down the hallway. It was coming from the front door. I saw the doorknob jiggling and heard another loud bang against the other side of the door. Somebody was trying to break into my place.

Frightened, I darted back down the hall and slammed and locked the bedroom door behind me. I shut off all the lights and swiped my phone off the bed before dashing to the back of my closet to call Rome. The phone rang and rang before eventually transferring over to his voicemail.

"Shit! Please pick up. Please pick up. Please pick up," I mumbled.

I hung up and dialed again and again until it stopped ringing altogether.

"Fuck!" I whispered as the phone shook in my shaky hands.

I threw on the closest top and bottom I could find without caring if they matched before I heard another loud bang. The sound of glass hitting the floor throughout the living room and kitchen area soon followed. Never letting my eyes leave the door, I felt around the pile of shoes I was hiding in and swept up a four-inch heel. It wasn't the best, but a weapon, nonetheless. Crouched down, I crawled to the front of the closet and pressed my ear against the door. I could hear two voices, one male and one female. One voice barked over the other as they argued, but I could only catch every other word. The clearer one of the voices became, the closer they edged down the hallway to my room. It was Draya. My heart skipped a beat. Had it been a stranger, my probability of survival would've been high, but I knew she was out for blood.

"Come out, come out wherever you are, bitch!" she threatened.

I scrambled back to the back of the closet when I heard them bump up against my bedroom door.

"That fuckin' bitch is in there! Knock that fuckin' door down, Cash! Do it! Do it right now!" Draya screamed.

"I got a better idea," he replied.

Everything fell silent for a few seconds before I heard a loud bang that couldn't have been mistaken for anything more than a gunshot. My shaking hands found their way over my mouth to drown out a scream. The bedroom door slammed against the closet, and they stalked inside. Hearing one crash after another, my ears lit up as they continued to rummage through my apartment, searching for me.

"That bitch ain't here," he declared, glancing around the closet without stepping inside. He let go of the handle, not allowing the door to clasp shut.

"How you know she ain't in there? You didn't even turn on the light," Draya fussed.

"You think I need a light to see if anyone is inside that little ass closet? The bitch ain't here."

"Then, where the fuck is she?"

"Maybe she at the fuckin' store or somethin', I don't know. You wanna sit and wait for her? We can do that. We can fuck on that

163

bitch's sheets if you want. I'm down for whatever," Cash told her before walking out of the room.

After I was sure they were down the hall, I quietly crawled out from the back of the closet and slid through the doorway's opening. I planned to jet over to the door, close and lock it to buy me enough time to climb out of my window and get away. As soon as I got out of the closet and reached for the bedroom door, I saw Draya standing in the doorway of the spare room with tears running down her cheeks. She turned her glossy eyes to me, and we both froze in place.

"What the fuck did you go back there for? I checked for the bitch back there," Cash yelled from the living room.

"I thought I heard something," she yelled back without tearing her eyes from mine.

"Well? You find anything?"

She looked down at my protruding belly and then at my face. "No. She's not back here. I think I'm ready to go."

"I thought this was what you wanted."

"I thought it was, but now I just want to go. Can we please go?" Draya asked him.

I slowly reeled back toward the window until my back was pressed against the pane. She stepped into the doorframe and stared at me. "Please, Draya—please let me go," I whispered.

"Go," she mouthed.

I lifted the windowsill and screen when I heard Cash's voice behind me. "What the fuck? Why are you letting this bitch go?"

"Lira, run!" Draya ordered.

I looked over my shoulder to see Cash charging toward me. I got half my body out of the window before he grabbed my ankle and tried to yank me back inside. I drew my free leg back and kicked as hard as possible while trying my best to protect my stomach. The kick sent him fumbling in reverse against the bed as he tried to regain his balance. I glanced back over my shoulder to see Draya holding him down long enough for me to scramble out of the window and run as fast as possible.

CASH

I cut my evil eyes at Draya. "I can't believe you let that bitch get away!"

"What can I say? I changed my mind."

"Changed your mind, huh?"

"Yeah, I changed my mind. Now can we just fuckin' go?"

"We'll go when I say we go!" I exploded.

"Excuse me?"

"You ain't never gonna be nothin' more than a manipulative ass bitch, you know that?"

"I don't know what you're talking about."

"Nah, fuck that. You are, and you know that shit! You're vindictive and manipulative enough to think that Rome would forgive your ass for what you did if you were the one who saved Lira and that baby from me. When you're the reason we're here in the fuckin' first place! You're the reason for all this shit, Dray!"

She twisted her lips. "You the one that fell in love, nigga! Talkin' about you'd do anything for me. You don't know the first thing about loyalty!"

"I don't know about loyalty? I came here for you! Ready to take a life for you! Ready to throw my life away and do time if it came down to it for you! I gave up the realest friendship I've ever had for you! You're the reason we're in all this shit, Dray! Because I can't fuckin' stay away from you! Can't you see you drive me fuckin' crazy? Huh? I'd give my life for you, but you standin' here talkin' to me tough like I won't kill us both!"

I stormed out of the room and into the kitchen to do a new line off the edge of the countertop.

"Cash, I wanna leave, now!" Draya exclaimed, barreling down the hallway.

I pulled up my shirt to highlight the gun on my waist. "Sit your fuckin' ass down."

Her eyes widened. It was the first time she ever looked at me with fear in her eyes, and it broke my heart to have to scare the woman I loved. But she'd crossed too many lines, and I was too emotionally scarred.

"W—what?"

"Grab your phone, Dray."

"Cash–"

"I said get your fuckin' phone!" The last thread of my thin patience snapped, and I pointed my gun at her. "Get that fuckin' phone and open your voice memos."

"Cash, no. I–"

"Somebody was gonna fuckin' die today. It was supposed to be Lira. You and I, we were supposed to prevail, Dray! Our love was supposed to come out on top, and now it's ruined. It's all fuckin' ruined," I mumbled as I typed a few sentences in the notes section on my phone and handed it to her. "Here's what you're gonna say, and don't leave out one fuckin' syllable."

"Baby, it's not ruined. Why can't we think of another way to get what we both want? Can we please? Let's talk about this!" she pleaded to deaf ears.

"Baby? Oh, now I'm your baby, right? When you ain't got shit left."

"It's you and me now, baby. We're all each other needs," Draya pleaded.

I knew she was scared. I smelled it radiating from her pores. "Have you ever loved me?" I asked. "Nah, you know what? Don't even say anything. We both know the answer, don't we? I think it's time we both stop lying to ourselves. It'll never work for us, Dray. Never."

"Cash, let's talk. We can talk about anything you wanna talk about. You wanna talk about us. Our future. Maybe even h—having another b—baby. We could be a real family, y'know? I just need you to p—put the gun down. We can't be a family when you have a gun pointed at me, baby."

"Stop! Just stop! You don't want a life with me! You don't want a family with me! You don't want shit but full control over me, Rome, Lira, and everything! All the games you played for all these months. All the hurdles you had me jumping over. All the fuckin' manipulative mind games and lies you've spun inside my head! All the times you—you know, you used to fuck me so good my dick would get stiff the next day just thinkin' about that pussy. No one's ever done that to me before."

"I'm sorry about everything, Cash. You're right. I have lied. I have been manipulative. I haven't been dealing with my feelings in the right way. I hurt you. I can see that now, and I'm sorry. You have to hear me when I say I am sorry."

"You ruined me, Dray. I am the monster you created, and I hate myself because of it!"

"What good will come from killing me? Huh? Nothing! All that will happen is that you'll end up going to jail! Do you want to spend the rest of your life in jail when you could be with me? Isn't that what you wanted?"

"If I thought even for a second that being with me was something you wanted, I'd walk right out of here with you today. But I know you, Dray. And I'd rather spend the rest of my life rotting in a cell before I let you spend the rest of yours pretending you love me."

Tears rolled down her cheeks like ocean waves. It seemed like she'd finally understood the magnitude of my love for her. Her body shook with fear as her misty eyes gazed into mine.

"I can't share you anymore, Dray. It hurts too much," I confessed. "Now read the words on the screen. I'm done talkin'."

Defeated, her hand trembled as she held her phone up to her lips, pressed record, and said the words I'd typed. "R–Rome is having an affair with Lira Armstrong. She's pregnant with his baby, and she wants to be with him. She's crazy obsessed with him, and I'm scared. I don't know what she's capable of."

"Good, now send that shit to your sister, your mother, Rome, and all your girls."

"Cash, please!"

I cocked my gun. "Is it sent?"

"I sent it."

"Don't fuck with me, Dray! Let me see it!"

She flashed the screen at me, showing me all her sent text messages. "I'm not. It's sent. I sent it! See?"

"Good. I love you, baby. I'm so fuckin' sorry it had to be this way."

"Cash, I—"

"Since I couldn't have you in this life, I'll see you in the next, baby," I told her before sending two bullets straight into her cold heart for shattering mine to pieces.

LIRA

A RUSH OF ADRENALINE SURGED THROUGH ME AS I RAN ACROSS THE parking lot and to a nearby shopping center. I darted inside the laundromat on the corner and headed straight to the back. I nervously pulled out my phone to call Rome again. No change. The next move I made was to get an Uber to take me to him. If he wasn't going to talk to me over the phone, he wouldn't be able to ignore me so easily face-to-face. I ran out of my apartment so fast; the only thing I did have was my phone. My keys, wallet, and everything else of value were probably in mid-torch by now.

Once in the backseat of my Uber, I rested my head against the headrest and closed my eyes. Draya's face immediately popped into my head. The conflict in her eyes was apparent. I had no idea why she let me go, but I was grateful she did. I exited my Uber and raced to Rome's front door, banging on it and ringing the doorbell like crazy. The door flew open, and Rome stood on the other side with his gun aimed and cocked. The rage in his eyes softened when he realized it was me causing the commotion.

"Why didn't you answer? I needed you! Why didn't you answer?" I screamed before windmilling my fists at his unwavering chest.

He tucked his gun away and grabbed both my flailing wrists. "Look, I've had a crazy fuckin' day, Lira, and I–I can't do this shit with you right now."

"They–They were trying to kill me, and I needed you to protect me. And you didn't answer!"

I followed his eyes to the table where his black iPhone screen lay smashed. "I broke my phone. What are you talking about? Who was trying to kill you?"

"Cash and Draya!"

Hearing their names made his heavy eyes perk up. "They did what to you?"

"They were at my apartment trying to kill me! Cash was going to kill me! They both were! I know it!"

"What?" he asked again, only that time he looked down at me. It was the first time he'd bothered to take a good look at me since he'd opened the door. I was shaking like a leaf on a tree and could barely string three sentences together.

"Both of them broke into my apartment and trashed it. I hid, and I was trying to make a run for it, and Draya caught me. She–she told me to run, and I was hanging out of the window kicking at Cash because he grabbed me by my ankles, and you weren't there! You didn't pick up. You didn't answer! I was scared, alone, and you weren't there!" I screamed.

He placed his hands on my shoulder. It was clear to see he was still trapped inside his mind. "I'm sorry, Lira. I'm so sorry for everything," he confessed before pulling me to his chest. "I will never let you go through something like that again."

"I hate you, Rome! I hate you so much that I love you!" I blabbed before locking my trembling arms around him.

His arms were the only place I wanted to be. They were the first place I thought about being when I got scared, and he was the first person I called, even before thinking of dialing 9-1-1. For better or for worse, Rome was my safe haven.

"Don't go back to that apartment. You're staying here with me from now on," he commanded.

"I don't feel comfortable with you going there either. I don't know what Cash is capable of!"

"I'll be okay."

I grabbed his wrists and held them tight. "Promise me," I demanded.

His look softened. "Okay."

"Say it. Say you promise!"

"I promise."

"You promise what?"

"I promise I won't go over there."

"Good."

"I can't believe that mothafucka went to your place! First Draya, now you. That nigga must have a death wish."

"None of it makes any sense to me."

"Why they came?"

"That, and why she let me go. She had me caught. She could've had Cash do anything she wanted him to do to me, but she didn't. She told me to run. I don't know if she's okay. I don't even know if I care, but the look in his eyes was crazy. I'd never seen anything like it before."

"He had the same look when he showed up here earlier this morning. He was wired as fuck and told me he was in love with my wife."

I flashed a round-eyed expression. His confession put so many things into perspective for me, validating the kiss I saw between them months ago, why Draya and Cash were together in the first place, and why she looked so unstable. Cash had blown up her happy little life by exposing her secret. "Oh shit."

"I went to bed last night with a wife and a best friend. I woke up this morning to them both becoming dead to me."

"How long has it been going on?" I asked with hesitance laced in my voice.

"He's been fuckin' her for months and been in love with her forever. It's so fucked-up that it's almost funny."

171

My brows sloped in confusion. "What's funny about any of this?"

"Because this entire time I've known you, I've been fighting. I've been fighting these raging, uncontrollable, damn near obsessive feelings for you. I was trying to do the right thing. I was trying to honor my vows, knowing my heart felt differently. I fought only for the two people I cared about most to rip my fuckin' heart right out of my chest. I looked out for her feelings and his pockets, and they both turned around and fucked me."

I reached up to hold his neck while looking into his eyes. "I'm so sorry...."

"What's there to be sorry for? I know someday I'll find the blessing in disguise in all of this shit."

"I know what it's like to have no one or lose someone you care about. That's what I'm sorry for. I'm not sorry that she cheated. I'm not sorry that they both lied. Because if it hadn't been for their actions, you never would've seen what I've been trying to tell you all along, that you can do so much better," I confessed.

"I know that now. Go lay down and try to get some rest. You're safe here."

"You don't think they'll come back here?"

"I think I made myself clear to both of them what would happen if they did."

I gave him a slow nod. "Are you going to look for them?"

"Don't worry about it anymore, Lira."

"What are you going to do to them when you do?"

He leaned down to kiss my forehead as he gently ran his hand across my stomach. "You two are the only good things I have left."

"That's not answering my question, Rome."

"That is me answering your question, Lira. You and my son are the only good things I have, which means I'll never share my bad side with you again."

I nodded. I'd seen what his bad side was capable of firsthand. "Okay."

Now that Rome and I were back under the same roof, I had to get a new wardrobe at his house since I'd never step foot back in that apartment again. Thinking about it still gave me chills. I was grateful to have Rome sleeping beside me at night, even if I knew a part of him was still torn up over Draya and Cash's betrayals. When it came to that, we had a don't ask, don't tell understanding. He wasn't in a space to talk about how brokenhearted he was over losing his best friend, and I wasn't in a space to hear him grieve out loud over his scandalous ass wife and where she was. I'd seen some crazy things in my life and the look in Cash's eyes that night made the top of my list. She'd be lucky if she made it out of there alive.

While I was staying in the apartment, Rome had taken it upon himself to have a decorator come in and do the baby's entire room, stocking it with diapers, clothes, wipes, and every other necessity. There was no doubt in my mind that he could handle fatherhood, but with Draya and Cash both MIA, I didn't feel right leaving him to his devices as a single parent. I'd been so attached to Rome, both physically and emotionally, that I hadn't considered moving to Cali in some time. For something that was once at the forefront of my mind, it almost seemed like a distant memory. I started getting more attached to the idea of keeping the baby and raising it with Rome. But staying meant putting my dreams on hold, and I didn't know if I was willing to sacrifice that again. Whether I decided to stay in Miami or not, I wanted the baby to have something special from me, so I put it on my to-do list to pick him up something when I went out to find something to wear for my graduation ceremony on Saturday.

After getting dressed, I walked around the house looking for Rome and found him sitting outside on the balcony, smoking a blunt and playing a game of chess against himself.

"Hey, you."

He twisted his neck in my direction. "Hey."

"Can I use the car? I want to go to the mall and find something to wear for my graduation this weekend, and I want to get something special for the baby," I told Rome.

"You want me to go with you? I can drive."

"No. You keep doing your thing. I'll be okay. I want to have a little me-time in the mall and do a little retail therapy," I told him.

"Aight. All the keys are on the key rack in the mudroom. Take whatever you want. Call me if you need me."

"Okay," I assured him before pecking his cheek. "I'll see you in a few hours."

Three hours later, I was shuffling out of the elevator and back out into the parking deck when my phone rang inside my purse. I paused, fishing around for it before I pressed accept and put it to my ear.

"Hello?"

"Hi. Is this Miss Lira Armstrong?" a female asked on the other end of the phone.

"This is she."

"Hi, Lira. My name is Mandy Owens. I'm a recruiter calling from the Cali Dance Studio in L.A. How are you today?"

Flabbergasted and eyes wide, I responded, "I'm doing great. And you?"

"Good. I was reviewing some of your videos submitted by one of your instructors, and I'm very impressed with your poise and technique. We've got a dance instructor job becoming available soon, and I'd like to invite you to apply, and see if we can get you out her to Cali for an in-person audition once you've officially graduated."

"W—wow! Really?"

"Yes, really. Now, I will say that the job does involve teaching students under the age of ten. Is that something you'd be interested in?"

My eyes bugged with excitement. "That would be amazing. Yes! Yes! I would love to."

I could practically hear her smiling through the phone. "Great, I'll be in touch in the coming weeks to set up your audition, okay?"

"That sounds good. Thank you so much for the opportunity!" I beamed.

"It's my pleasure. Talk soon."

"Thanks, bye."

I ended the call with a smile on my face just as I approached the car. After going through that crazy ordeal with Cash and Draya, I was excited that good things were finally starting to align for me. As soon as I unlocked the door, I heard someone call out my name.

"Lira Armstrong?"

I turned to see a swarm of police cars and SWAT pulled up and surrounded me. Dozens of men in uniform raced from their vehicles with guns aimed in my direction. Naturally, I dropped everything I had and put my hands up.

"Lira Armstrong?" an armored man called out again.

My lips trembled. "Y—yes."

"You're under arrest for the murder of Draya Snow."

"What? S—she's dead?" I quizzed as they twisted my arms behind my back and slapped metal cuffs around my wrists.

"You have the right to remain silent. Anything you say can and will be used against you in a court of law. You have the right to an attorney. If you cannot afford an attorney, one will be provided. Do you understand the rights I have read to you?" the arresting officer asked me.

"Yes! I understand, but you have to listen to me! It wasn't me! It wasn't me! I swear it wasn't me!" I screamed as they pressed the crown of my head down and put me inside the back of the cop car. I kicked and screamed, pleading for someone to listen to what I said as the cars pulled off one by one. I twisted my neck out of the window to see the customized onesie and receiving blanket I'd gotten for the baby crumpled up on the pavement.

ROME

With Lira out of the house, I had a couple of hours to figure out where Draya and Cash ran off to. Not only did they betray me, but they threatened the life of my unborn son. I couldn't let that go unpunished. I kept my word to Lira and didn't go back to her apartment. Instead, I went into my office and pulled up the security camera footage from the cameras I had installed in her apartment. I wanted to see precisely what happened or maybe get a clue about where Draya and Cash went next. I watched footage from the living room and Lira's bedroom and was sick to my stomach. I raced to the bathroom and threw up everything in my system—flashbacks of what I'd witnessed flashed in my head, one scene after the other. I watched Cash put two bullets in Draya's chest and drag her body down the hallway and into Lira's bathroom. He walked out a few minutes later, following the trail of her blood back to the living room where he shot her, then walked out of the front door as if nothing had happened.

After rinsing out my mouth and getting myself together, I called Chief and Baby to come over. At that point, Cash was an enemy and a loose cannon. One minute he was standing at my front door confessing his love for my wife, and then the next, I watched him murder her in cold blood. There was no telling what he would do next. When my brothers arrived, the first thing I did was show them the footage. They were as stunned as I was to witness Cash in action.

"Damn, that man done lost his mind," Baby muttered. "Why the fuck would he kill Dray?"

"He was in love with her," I announced, dropping the first of many bombs.

"What?" Baby yelled.

"They were fuckin' behind my back. The baby she lost could've easily been his."

Chief's eyes widened, and I could tell he was thinking about things from a business standpoint. "What the fuck you gon' do about this?"

"I don't know what to do with this shit. I can't go to the cops about it. I have to handle it myself.

"I agree it's a delicate situation, but I think the first thing y'all need to do is move your product," Chief proposed.

Baby nodded. "He's right. He knows where all our stashes are, and he has access to them."

"That nigga is a wild card right now. You don't know if he's gon' go to the cops to have your shit raided or try to rob it himself. You said he looked like he was on something when he showed up here, right?" Chief asked.

"Yeah.

"And he looked out of his fuckin' mind in that video. You can't trust that nigga," Baby added.

Chief looked at me and then wagged his head. "What's that shit Meek said? Niggas wanna burn a bridge and expect you to send a yacht. He fucked your wife behind your back. That's your rib, nigga. You gon' have to put 'em down."

"That's two bodies on me in less than a year. I've never been sweet, but that's now how I get down," I told him.

"I respect that shit, I do. But tell me, what's the alternative? Draya's dead. She's gone. He tried to hurt your unborn son. It's la familia for life, remember? He's no longer our family, Rome. He's the enemy. We go to the furthest extent to protect our family from our enemies, don't we?"

I tipped my head forward. "Yeah, we do."

"Hell yeah, we do," Baby joined in.

"The truth is, this nigga has the power to jeopardize the plate that you're preparing to go on the table in front of your unborn son. He's putting our family in jeopardy. Marrying Draya was your first mistake. Don't let not dealing with Cash be your second. You have to put him down," he warned.

I tore my eyes over to Baby, who nodded in agreeance with Chief. "Ain't no other way around it."

It broke my heart to have my closest friend, somebody I considered another brother, turn his back on me. When it came to my business and money, not much got past me. But when it came to my heart, Lira had consumed so much of my attention that I didn't see what was going on right under my nose between my best friend and my wife. I'd always considered Draya a beast that couldn't be tamed, but staring into the kaleidoscope of reality, I saw her true colors were always there. I was too color blind to notice. Cash, he was different, though. He'd always been my ace. My right hand. My homie. Now, he was a stranger. What my brothers were saying was true. The level of betrayal was astounding. He couldn't be trusted. He was a wild card. He did and still was putting my family in jeopardy. When it came time to pull that trigger, the only voice that would matter was my own.

Baby reached out and placed his hand on my shoulder. "You know we got you, right?"

I nodded while dapping him up. "'Til the death."

Baby and I split up the work, deciding which of us would hit which stash house to move product, while Chief worked on changing the codes to the bunker and anything else Cash had access to. As I was making my rounds, collecting and moving product, I hit up my lawyer for advice on what to do about Draya. By law, she was my wife, and if anybody got to her body before I did, I knew all eyes would be on me.

"Hello?" he answered.

"We need to speak privately. Is now a good time?"

"Roman, I'm glad you called."

"I need to talk to you about Draya. She's dead."

"I know," he responded.

My forehead puckered. "What? How'd you know?"

"You haven't been contacted by the police yet?"

"Contacted for what?"

"Oh shit, Roman," he mumbled before the line went silent.

"What?"

"I'm sorry to have to be the one to tell you this, but Lira was arrested for Draya's murder about an hour ago. The neighbors called the police when they heard gunshots and other commotion. When the police arrived, they found Draya's body inside the bathtub. She'd been shot multiple times."

"Man, fuck!" I exploded. Lira's arrest was another thing tacked onto my list of things to handle.

"I'm sorry, Roman."

"Listen, I need you to represent her."

"What?"

"She's innocent, and I can get you the proof you need. I'm out right now, though. Just promise me you'll represent her. I'll pay you whatever retainer fee you require."

"And you're sure she didn't do it?"

"I'm positive," I confirmed while putting the last duffel bag of product into the backseat of my G-Wagon.

"Okay. I'll get down to the station and see what I can find out. I'll be in touch."

I nodded. "As soon as you can find out anything, let me know—"

I stopped mid-sentence when I heard a familiar voice call out behind me. "You took everything from me!"

I swiveled my neck to see Cash walking up to me with a gun aimed right at my head. "Yo, Cash. Don't do this here, I–"

POW! POW! POW! POW!

My body hit the ground in one loud thud, and the phone fell to my side.

"Rome? Rome! Can you hear me? Are you there? Stay on the phone with me! I'm calling 9-1-1," I heard my lawyer calling out through the receiver. My eyes rolled back in my head before they closed and didn't reopen.

LIRA

IT WASN'T ME. I SWEAR IT WASN'T ME, WERE THE ONLY WORDS MY BRAIN would allow me to say as they marched me into the jail for booking with a trail of warm tears streaming down my cheeks. The officers wasted no time starting the intake process. First came my mugshot, and then they took my fingerprints. Then, I was led into a room and told to strip down for a full body search, so any tattoos or body piercings could be documented in my file.

"I see you are pregnant, ma'am," the female officer stated.

I nodded as I sniffed. "Yes."

"How far along?"

"Um, I'm in my third trimester," I answered.

"How far along?" she repeated. "In *weeks*?"

"Thirty."

The female officer nodded and walked over to take all my personal property and clothing before grabbing a two-piece black uniform for me to put on. "Here," she said before sitting behind the computer to click her coffin-shaped nails against the keyboard. "Any gang affiliation?" she inquired.

My brows wrinkled. "What? No."

"Kill the attitude, ma'am. These questions are procedural. Any relationships with any gang members?" she continued.

"I said no. Can't you see I'm pregnant and all fucked-up right now? Do I look like I could be involved in a gang?"

"Again, it's protocol, ma'am. The quicker you answer, the quicker we can both move on. Pregnant or not, the sun does not rise and fall on your ass. Now, are you on any medications?"

I sighed. "Only prenatal vitamins."

"Next of kin?"

With every question that rolled off her tongue, an anxiety attack brewed in the pit of my stomach, revving up like a tornado in the Midwest. Every muscle in my body began to wind tight. My forehead and armpits became instantly drenched in stress-triggered sweat, and my heart felt like it would leap out of my chest. Fresh tears began spilling down my face as I grabbed my chest.

"I said, next of kin," the officer repeated.

As dizzy and discombobulated as I was, I looked at her before turning my attention to the open door. There was an alarming feeling in my stomach telling me to run. If I was in a fight or flight scenario, I chose to fly. I jutted toward the door, trying my best to escape the spinning room and flee the jail and the waking nightmare I'd been sucked into. I was swiftly apprehended, kicking, and screaming once more.

"No!" I screamed. "It's a mistake! This is all a horrible mistake! Please, you have to believe me! I don't know what happened to Draya! I swear I didn't kill her!"

"Ma'am, calm down, or we will have to sedate you," a male officer told me as another one stood there holding my squirming shoulders in his arms.

"No! You don't understand! I shouldn't be here! I didn't do anything wrong! My college graduation is this Saturday! This is all one big mistake!"

"Ma'am, calm down!" the officer said with a stilted tone that let me know it wouldn't take much effort on his part to break me in two.

"Okay, okay. Just...give me some water, please. I—I need to catch my breath," I panted.

One officer brought over a Styrofoam cup of water and handed it to me. I sipped slowly, trying to regain my calm while they watched me like a hawk. I nervously spilled droplets of water down the front of my uniform as I struggled to hold the cup steady inside my trembling grasp.

With a tension filled expression across my face, I asked, "So, what happens to me now?"

"We'll house you with the other pregnant inmates once your processing is complete," the officer who handed me the water answered.

"And that's it? You're going to leave me in a cell?"

"Yes, until your arraignment. Then, you'll be able to get a public defender or your own lawyer and wait for your official hearing date," the female officer replied.

Hearing the words fall off her lips caused the waterworks to start again as I marched down the long corridor to an eight-by-eight square cell. It had a flat panel bed secured to the concrete wall with a foam mattress on top, like the ones they use for kids in daycare, and a pillow that looked about as soft as a concrete block. In the corner, there was a desk built into the wall, a chair, and a steel toilet and sink with a small square mirror above it.

"Welcome home," the escort told me before the thick, white door closed, locking itself behind him.

The door had a small square window to look out of and a section where food could be served without a guard physically opening the door. There was also a rectangular window with four vertical bars over it, obstructing any chance I had at a glimpse of the outside world. The entire room smelled like stale piss and utter fuckin' hopelessness. The noisy sound of locks snapping around me every few minutes was enough to push me past the point of breaking. I edged myself onto the foam mattress and buried my head in my palms. The baby was jumping around and kicking inside me with such force that I knew he could feel that something terrible was happening in the outside world.

"Please settle down, baby boy. Please, please settle down. We're going to be okay. I'm going to figure this shit out; I promise you I will," I whispered as I ran my hand back and forth over my belly.

Truthfully, I had no fuckin' clue how I could be linked to Draya's murder. A million different scenarios bubbled up in my mind. I wondered if Rome knew anything about me being arrested or what happened to his wife. He was the only person who could attest to me not knowing shit about Draya's whereabouts unless he was trying to get me caught up. He knew the last time I saw her, she was alive and telling me to get out of my apartment with my own life. Cash had to have killed her, but I never saw any of that shit pointing back to me. Or maybe it was Rome's way of getting back at me for not telling him about Jevan and Bankx's plan whenever Bankx got out of prison. Whatever it was, I had to find a way to get myself out of jail so that I wouldn't risk having my baby behind bars. Forty-five minutes passed before I heard the lock snap and the door open.

"Let's go," the officer commanded.

I slowly rose to my feet. "W—where are we going?"

"Walk."

His fingertips pinched the inside of my arm as he guided me down one long corridor after another.

"Ow! You're hurting my arm!"

"I said walk!"

I was so tired of people pushing me around and telling me when to go and how to get there. I could tell he took pleasure in being difficult. Some people relied on caffeine to get them through their day; others ran on pure hate. I wanted answers not only because I deserved them but also because I was innocent. Somebody needed to start painting a clear picture for me to figure out what the hell my next move would be.

"Can I make a phone call? What about a lawyer? I need a lawyer," I declared before being shuffled behind a door.

He flipped the light switch, illuminating an empty visitation room. I marched to the table, where he forced me to sit down. He cuffed my wrist to the table as if I could successfully wobble my pregnant ass right out the front door. Without pushing out another word, he turned and left. The door opened again before I had time to think, revealing a familiar face. As lovely as Agent Martinez's face and tattoos were to look at, he was the last person I wanted to see.

"Lira," he stated.

I drew my eyes up to his. "Why am I here? I didn't do anything!"

"You're here because of your relationship with Roman Snow and his now-deceased wife, Draya Snow."

"Look, I don't know what you think happened, but I *didn't* kill Draya. I don't know how many times I have to say it! The last time I saw her, she was alive!"

"And when exactly was that?"

I clasped my hands together to stop them from shaking. "A week ago maybe. She showed up at my apartment, her and another guy. They broke in. He looked crazy, and she looked scared."

"Who was the guy Draya was with?"

"Rome's best friend, Cash," I confessed.

Agent Martinez sat back in his chair, swirling the plastic stirrer inside his coffee mug. "And then what happened?"

"He—he was aggressive. Enraged, even. There was this crazed look in his eyes like he was on something. I'm telling you he had something to do with it. He didn't look stable. She told me to run, so I got out through the bedroom window. I didn't see her anymore after that, so I don't know what happened. I'm telling you that she was alive the last time I saw her!"

"If that's true, then why was Draya's body found inside your apartment, and why did we find this recording on Draya's phone saying if anything happened to her, you were the one that did it?"

My eyes shot open. "W—what? No. No! That's not what happened at all. You'll hear I'm telling you the truth if you listen!"

"Or maybe you should be the one to take a listen," he said, pulling out a recorder and pressing play. I heard Draya's voice alleging that I was the one who was obsessed with her husband and that if anything happened to her, all roads would point to me. When the recording finished, he shot me a questioning look. "Are you ready to tell me the truth now?"

"I've already told you the truth! None of this makes any sense to me! What did I kill her with? Huh? Where's the weapon? Where are my fingerprints?"

"Let me paint a picture for you. You meet. He's charming, and he's paid. The only problem is, he's married. So, you try to think of another way to get him to be with you. Even after you became pregnant with his baby, that's still not enough to keep him. You wanted to be with Roman so bad that you'd do anything so that you two could be a family with your unborn baby, even if it meant taking his wife's life. She sent that message to multiple people and then all of a sudden mysteriously winds up dead in your apartment. What else am I supposed to think?"

I protested, shaking my head enthusiastically. He didn't know how wrong he was. All those years and money wasted on school and education, and he still didn't know shit. A single, frustrated tear slipped down my cheek.

"I didn't do it."

"And what about Jevan? Are you still expecting me to believe that you had nothing to do with that either?"

There he went again, tossing out Jevan's name and trying to force a reaction out of me. "I already told you I don't know nothin' about him, where's he's at, where's he's not, nothing."

He twisted his lips to the side before down turning his brow. "You're going to start having to give me answers about something. You can't protect him forever."

"I'm not protecting anyone but myself!" I hailed.

I watched his head take a sharp slice left then right. "All of this for a man who doesn't give a damn about you."

My forehead puckered. "Excuse me?"

"Think about it, Lira. Where is he now while you're in here? You're looking at a first-degree murder charge. That's you behind bars for years. You'll be lucky if you see that baby you're carrying walk across the stage at its college graduation."

He tried to get in my head and set me up to admit to something I had no part in. As mentally distressed as I was, there was no way I would let him win. My lungs expelled all the air inside my anxiety-filled chest. I sucked in a quick breath through my teeth, touching my lower back. The pain had been coming in different forms all day. It started as dull and unnoticeable when I woke up, progressed to quick and sharp, and then settled down again.

"Are you okay?"

"Mmhm."

A second later, a lean white man walked in with a briefcase in hand and a pair of bottle cap glasses over his eyes. "Can me and my client have the room?"

Agent Martinez frowned. "Client? Since when?"

"Since now, Agent Martinez. I'm a busy man, and I bill by the hour, so if you don't mind."

I was too focused on getting my mind off the pain shooting through my back that I didn't notice him walk out or the lawyer sit down.

"Miss Armstrong?"

"Yeah."

"I'm Drew Friedman."

"Are you really my lawyer?"

He uttered a hushed laugh. "Yes. I'm your lawyer. I'm Roman's lawyer and have been for some time now. He is the one who called to put me on your case."

My ears perked up at the mention of Rome. "Have you heard from him? Does he know I'm here? They haven't let me call anyone."

He lowered his head. "Yes, but before we get into that, I think it's important that I give you an update on your situation."

"Okay."

"I want us to have a successful attorney-client relationship like the one I have with Roman. Now, this meeting is more like an intake. I won't do repeated jail visits, but you will receive weekly letters from my office on the status of your case."

"Wait, you're not here to take me home? I—I can't get bail or anything? I have to stay here?"

"You're being charged with first-degree murder, Lira. The prosecutors will try and prove that Draya's murder was premeditated on your part. They will question the paternity of your child. Once they know it's Roman's baby, that will give you motive. Your family over hers."

I sighed explosively. Shit was not looking good for me. "But I didn't murder anyone! I don't even think I'm capable of something like that!"

"That may be true, but do you know where her body was found?"

"He told me they found her body in my apartment, but I didn't do it. I swear I didn't! I put that on my life. Rome can prove it! I left and went straight to him, and I haven't been back to that apartment since!"

"First-degree murder is a serious charge, Lira. Whether you did it or not, I am not here to judge. We need to change what they think you did and how they think you did it. I'm working now to get the evidence. Once I receive it, I'll come and meet with you again, and we'll go over everything together. This way, you have a chance to ask any questions you may have."

"How long do you think I'll have to be in here?"

"Your hearing hasn't been scheduled yet, but I expect it to be done in the coming weeks," he stated.

My heart sunk to the pit of my stomach. *"Weeks?* I have to be in here for weeks? How many? One? Two?"

He sloped his head to the left. "I don't know."

"I don't think you understand. I'm in my third trimester. The countdown is on until this baby's due date in a matter of weeks. I can't have my baby in –ah! I—I can't have my baby in j—jail. Ah!" I squealed as the sharp pain in my back intensified.

"That's the worst-case scenario. I'm giving you all the facts so you know what to expect looking ahead."

"Okay."

"Are you okay?"

I massaged my lower back before nodding. "Y—yeah."

He eyed me in silence before starting up again. "When I leave here today, don't call me to speak about your case. The calls are recorded and monitored here, and I don't accept them. I can also promise you they will be reviewed by that jerk, Agent Martinez. He's had it out for the Snow family for a while, trying to take down one brother after another. He will do anything to get you to say or do anything that will incriminate Roman and his family. So, the next time he presents himself to you, the only thing you need to tell him is that you want to speak to me."

"Okay."

"Our communications are considered private, and they are protected by law. What we speak about, I cannot tell a soul. Everything is confidential, okay? So, there's no need to worry. Start by telling me about your relationship with Roman. How'd you two meet? And when did you meet his wife?"

My mind flashed back to the first time I laid eyes on Roman Snow. He had a gun pointed at my face. Deep in thought, I realized how he'd gone from taking a life to putting a life inside me. The white man seated in front of me had done his best to share comforting words to make the inside of the room feel like a safe space to share the convoluted details of my relationship, but all I wanted to do was talk to Rome.

"Can you get word to Rome that I'm okay? I mean, obviously, he knows I'm here. I thought I'd be going home. This is all one big ass nightmare that I can't seem to wake up from," I vented.

"Lira, I need to tell you something about Roman."

"What?"

"He was shot."

My heart collapsed. "Shot? H—how is he? Is—is he okay?"

"I'm going to be honest with you. I don't know. When the altercation happened, I was on the phone with him, and I called 9-1-1. I stayed on the phone long enough to hear when the paramedics arrived, but someone disconnected the call. I don't know if he survived."

I clasped my hand over my mouth, feeling the kind of pain that was unendurable. "Oh my God!"

My heart rate escalated. The agony was so pronounced that it blocked out everything else in my mind until the pain itself was all I could think about. I couldn't bear the thought of losing someone else. I just couldn't.

"Lira, are you okay?"

A piercing throb shot through my lower back, followed by two more of the same intensity a few minutes later. "Ah!" I winced in distress.

"Lira!"

A quick no jerked my head before I gripped my back. It felt like someone was ripping my spine out of my body. "No. I—I think something is—something is wrong with the b—baby."

His blue eyes widened with concern. "Can we get some help in here!" the lawyer yelled.

Two guards rushed over to me as I scrunched my body into the fetal position. *Please, God, don't let this be early labor,* I silently prayed. I overheard the guard on his walkie-talkie calling for backup. They shuffled me outside in a stretcher and into the back of an ambulance. Then another shooting pain came. And another. And then another one after that. And they kept coming every fifteen seconds. It was a feeling I'd never felt before, and as time went on, it only got more and more intense.

"It hurts! It h—hurts s—so bad," I sobbed to the EMT.

"Ma'am, can you tell me how far along you are?"

"I—I don't know. I'm, I'm in my th—third trimester," I uttered.

I was so frantic about what was happening to me, that the fact that I was only thirty weeks along failed to come out of my mouth.

"And can you tell me how far apart your contractions are and when they started?"

"They are fi—fifteen seconds. E—every fif—fifteen seconds," I stuttered. "Is my baby going to be okay? It's too soon!"

"We'll get you to labor and delivery, where they will do their best to stop your contractions, okay? Right now, I need you to try and relax."

My eyes tracked over to the officer who was along for the ride during my transport to the hospital. I tried to read his facial expressions to get an idea of what was going on. He didn't look worried, and he didn't look unflustered either.

"Can somebody please let me know what is happening with my baby?" I pleaded while tugging at the officer's pant leg.

"Don't touch me, inmate!" he dictated as he shooed me away like a pest.

"Ma'am, I need you to stay calm. We'll get you some answers as soon as you get admitted," the EMT advised.

Defeated, I closed my eyes and tried to focus on stabilizing my breathing until we made it to the hospital. The closer we got, the more intense and frequent my contractions seemed to get. When we arrived at the hospital, they rolled me into the elevator and took me to the high-risk labor and delivery unit. Nurses ran around everywhere, hooking me up to all types of machines and monitors, taking bloodwork, and checking my cervix. I continued to have contractions that were seconds apart through it all.

"Is my baby okay?" I probed.

"Ma'am, you're two centimeters dilated and in active labor. We will give you magnesium to try and stop the labor and some medicine to help get your contractions under control. We're also going to give your baby a steroid for his lungs to help them develop faster, okay?"

I was numb from the waist down an hour later, thanks to the epidural. Even though the drug managed to minimize my misery, everything was still happening at warp speed. Julia, the head nurse, walked in to give me an update.

"Lira, how are you feeling now that you've gotten the epidural?"

I nodded before pulling the oxygen mask off my face. "I feel a lot better."

"I'm glad you're comfortable, but unfortunately, your contractions couldn't be medically stopped, and you're still dilating."

My fingers trembled as I clasped them together. "What does that mean?"

"It means we cannot stop your labor. You are going to have this baby today," she said plainly.

My eyes prickled with tears. "It's not time for him to come yet. Is he fully developed? Will he be okay?"

She flashed me a sincere look. "Your son will be born prematurely. We won't be able to access his condition until he's delivered. Since his major organs haven't finished developing, he may have issues eating or breathing for a few weeks. But don't worry, we'll keep him in the NICU and monitor him around the clock. Once he starts to put on weight and can breathe on his own, then he should be cleared to go home if he stays on track. You don't panic until we panic, okay?"

I nodded. She was the first person all day that talked to me like I was an actual human being. "Okay, thank you. I'm scared, but I feel better now."

The nurse reached down to check my cervix. "Oh my God."

"What's wrong?" I asked.

"Get the doctor in here now! We need to get her to the operating room now!" she screamed.

My eyes flashed open wide with fear. "What's wrong?"

It was insanity from that point on. The nurse discovered that the baby's umbilical cord was hanging out of my cervix and cutting off his oxygen supply. The doctor rushed into the room with three nurses trailing closely behind him.

"How are the baby's vital signs?" he asked.

"The baby is in distress. His heart rate keeps dropping, and we can't get Mom's blood pressure to stabilize either," one nurse reported.

"Doctor, she's ten centimeters dilated, and one hundred percent effaced. She's ready to push," said another.

Everything was going wrong. I locked eyes with the nurse standing closest to me. The terror in her eyes mirrored mine. "I'm so scared," I told her.

"Okay, Lira. We're going to get this baby out right now. Are you ready to push?" the doctor asked me.

I froze. The funny thing about big moments is that you can rehearse how you'll react every day in your head for weeks on end, what you'll say, how you'll look. How much it'll hurt. Which one of you, the baby will favor most. And then the moment comes, and it's nothing like you expect because life *always* has other plans.

"Okay, first push on three. One...two...three...push!" The doctor hailed, slamming me back into the present.

I pressed my chin to my chest and pushed down toward my bottom.

"Push as hard as you can, okay? One...two...and three...push!"

The sweet sound of his first cry pierced my ears four pushes later. Tears of joy slid from the corners of my eyes. The nurses whisked him to the NICU before I even got a chance to see his face.

ROME

"Welcome back, Mr. Snow," a raspy male voice called out to me. "Can you hear me?"

My eyelids fluttered softly as I opened my eyes. I squinted in confusion only able to fully see out of one eye. My vision was still slightly blurry in the other. Waking up felt like emerging from the depths of the ocean. I remembered being rushed to the emergency room in an ambulance and getting a CAT scan before everything went black. The next thing I saw was Lira and our son as if nothing terrible had happened to either of us.

"Can you hear me, Mr. Snow?" the voice called out again.

I nodded my head slowly, mouth too dry to part my lips. Then, I raised my hand to touch my left eye, feeling a gauze bandage covering it.

"I'm Dr. William Harrow. You are under my care inside the hospital's intensive care unit. Do you remember anything about how you got here?"

I slowly turned my neck from left to right, although I remembered

195

everything perfectly. Before I blacked out, I promised myself that if God saw fit to keep my left titty beatin', I'd put Cash down like the dog he was the next time I saw him.

"You were shot multiple times at close range by a gunman police are still trying to locate. While all the injuries you sustained were flesh wounds only and will heal, one of those bullets grazed your left cornea. We had to fly in the best surgeons to do reconstructive surgery on your left eye, and although we were able to save it, you have lost thirty percent of your sight in that eye. We put you in a medically induced coma for a few days to help with the healing and preserve as much function in your body as possible. The good news is, with the right therapy and some more corrective surgeries in your future, we *may* be able to restore some of your sight after you've had efficient time to heal, but I can't make any promises, of course."

I grunted as a single tear slipped down the side of my face. Although thankful I still had my life; I was enraged. It didn't matter if that doctor had declared me legally blind; Cash tried to take my life from me and failed. I wasn't gon' stop until I walked 'em down. My right eye oscillated around the room, taking in the devoid of life outside of the doctor and me.

"W—where's my wife?" I asked.

He took his eyes down to the ground. "Do you not remember, Mr. Snow?"

"Remember what?"

"I'm so sorry to have to be the one to tell you this, but your wife was murdered weeks ago. The funeral is in a few days," Dr. Harrow informed me.

His words immediately triggered my brain's response as images of Lira's face instantly flooded my mind. I was never talking about Draya. The best part of being in a coma was my dream with Lira as my wife and our son by my side. It felt so real that I could've sworn it was an actual memory I had experienced.

"I want to speak to my lawyer," I stated.

He bobbed his head. "I understand that, Mr. Snow, but I feel that you need to know the recovery time ahead of you. We'll need to keep you under close monitoring for the next week or so to ensure all your vitals stay within a healthy range and make sure that your body isn't reacting in a way that it shouldn't be before you can be discharged. Our goal is to ensure that you return to optimal function as quickly and as safely as possible."

Before I could respond, we shifted our attention to the knock on the door. A man flashed his badge in the doctor's direction. "FBI Special Agent Miguel Martinez. I'm here to question Mr. Snow about the death of his wife, Draya. Can I please have the room?"

"He's in no shape, physically or mentally, to undergo questioning. He barely knows what happened to him. It may take him a few days to become fully aware of his surroundings."

"Can I have the room, doctor?" he repeated, not givin' a fuck about my condition.

Doctor Harrow let out a blistering sigh before exiting the room. Agent Martinez slowly made his way over to my bedside. "Roman Snow, as I live and breathe."

I squinted my eye at him, refusing to open my lips. In my mind, I wanted to tell his ass to get the fuck out of my face, but I knew better than to exert what limited strength I did have on his ass.

"The moment I heard you were awake, I decided that now was good of a time to visit you and ask you a few questions about your wife's death. You must be so heartbroken."

My arms felt too weak to move away from my side, but I managed to pull my right hand up to run my fingers over my dry lips.

I craned my neck in the opposite direction. "Then, why the fuck you ain't lettin' me grieve in peace?" I mumbled.

"Your wife is dead, and someone tried to put you in the grave next to her. What kind of enemies have you made, Mr. Snow?"

I didn't even consider giving him a response. If he was gon' disrespect me and continue to be a part of the problem, I'd be damned if I showed him any respect in return. If my mouth didn't feel like cotton, I would've spat on his ass.

"Well?" he asked.

"Don't say a damn thing to him, Roman," my lawyer called out upon entering my private hospital room.

"Mr. Friedman. We will have to stop meeting like this," Agent Martinez greeted him.

"And yet, I find you here harassing my client after he's woken up from a traumatic experience. Is there no such thing as dignity in your line of profession anymore, Agent Martinez?" my middle-aged, freckle-faced lawyer asked.

Agent Martinez turned to me. "We'll talk some other time."

"I've been askin' for you," I told my lawyer when the two of us were alone.

"I know. Your doctor called and told me before telling me that prick was in here trying to question you. Luckily, I was already here when I got the call."

"Here? Why were you already here? How are Lira and my son? Have you spoken to my brothers?" I asked, barely pausing from one question to the next.

"Yes, I've spoken to Dominic, and he assured me he'd let your other brother know your status. As for Lira and the baby, well, they're the reason I'm here, Rome. I was down at the jail giving her an update on her court hearing and letting her know that you were shot and, in a coma, when she started clutching her stomach and screaming in anguish. The paramedics and guards rushed in and brought her here for an emergency delivery."

"What the fuck?! Is she okay? It's too early for her to have him. Is my son okay? I need to go them!"

"Calm down, Roman. I'm sorry, but you are in no shape to go anywhere. You look like you barely have enough strength to hold your head up. I couldn't get too much information, but I do know that the delivery was successful and that your son has been placed in the NICU since he was born prematurely. I don't know her status yet, but I will go and check on her and let you know something as soon as I do."

"Man, fuck!" I growled, pissed off for feeling helpless as a lamb. "I need to see my son, and I need to make sure Lira is okay."

"And all that will happen in time, Rome. Not right now. Not in your condition. For now, I'll be your eyes and ears, and you focus on getting your body back to functioning at one hundred percent."

A defeated sigh pushed past my flaring nostrils as I tried to clench my fist as tight as possible. "Aight."

LIRA

I NEVER IMAGINED I'D DELIVER MY CHILD ALONE AND WITH MY WRIST shackled to a hospital bed. Even in a moment as traumatic and beautiful as giving birth to my son, the correctional officer assigned to me still stood guard outside my hospital door as if I was a serial killer who had to be watched every waking moment. When I was about to press the call button for the nurse, there was a knock on the door and then a back-and-forth conversation between the guard and whoever was trying to get in to see me. A few moments later, the lawyer walked in wearing a collared, white polo shirt and golf shoes as if he'd spent his morning enjoying the nineteenth hole.

"Lira! I came down as soon as I heard you were here and had the baby. How are you feeling? They said you had an emergency delivery."

I bobbed my head. "Yeah."

"How is the baby doing?"

I shook my head. "I don't know. No one barely tells me anything. I know that he was born prematurely, and after they delivered him, they shipped him straight to the NICU. It's been hours, and I haven't even gotten the chance to hold him, see his face, or sniff his skin. He doesn't even have a name," I confessed.

I missed my son, and I hadn't even officially met him yet. I missed Rome. I needed him to be the person I became unhinged in front of, but the lawyer would have to do. The assembly line of tears poured from my eyes one after another. I thought only a man had the power to crush my heart until motherhood fell into my lap. It was a feeling I'd never experienced before. I was baffled at how I could feel empty and so full at the same time.

"I'm so sorry about all of this, Lira. I'll see what I can find out for you, but I have good news."

"Am I going to walk out of here with my baby and without the handcuffs?" I quizzed.

"Not quite."

"Then, there's no other news that could be better than that, so save it."

"It's about Rome. He's awake!" he exclaimed.

My heart somersaulted in my chest. "W—what?"

"He wants to see you, but certain things prevent that right now."

"Things like what?"

He sighed as if he knew the news he was about the share wouldn't put a smile on my face. "One of the injuries he sustained was from a bullet that grazed his left cornea. The doctors had to do reconstructive surgery, and he ended up losing thirty percent of his sight in that eye."

My hand cupped my mouth. Although I was grateful to hear that he had survived and was out of his coma, I was still scared to death.

"Did you hear what I said?" he confirmed.

"I did, and I'm still scared."

He shrugged his sculpted shoulders. "Sometimes fear can be a good thing. This is all new, and everything is changing so rapidly. If you weren't, I might think something was wrong with you."

His quirky response brought a bud of a smile to my face.

"When are you going to check in on the baby for me?"

"I dropped by the NICU to see if I could speak with your nurse or doctor before coming to your room, but even lawyers have limits. I was able to get a picture of him on my phone that I can show you. I'll speak with them again, though. They can't withhold information about your child's health, no matter the circumstances."

Friedman pulled up the picture and handed his phone to me. I took one look at the picture, and a fresh set of tears emptied from my tired obs. He was the spitting image of Rome, from his complexion down to the shape of his lips and nose.

"Oh my God! He's beautiful," I wailed. "He's so beautiful."

"He's a fighter. I can see it in his eyes," he replied.

"Wait, if Rome and I are both in the hospital, who will the baby go with once the doctors discharge him?"

"Don't worry. We're focused on getting Rome back on his feet and getting you cleared of all charges against you. But if none of that happens before the time the doctors say your son is well enough to leave the hospital; I'll make sure he is in a comfortable home. I'll talk to Rome about it, but we'll likely plan for him to go with Rome's next of kin, his older brother Dominic."

"Do you think I'll be able to see him before they take me back to—j—jail?"

He rested his pale hand on my shoulder. "I'll see what I can do."

ROME

THREE WEEKS LATER.

After being discharged from the hospital, I spent the last few weeks getting to know my son through an incubator and trying to get used to wearing sunglasses or a patch over my eye whenever I was in public while my eye continued to heal. Even without having my full vision, I was still allowed to get around like I used to with little to no assistance. If I wasn't with one of my brothers, I was at the hospital. I started processing death differently once I got shot. I'd faced death a lot over the years. It was the only thing in life that was certain. Inevitable. I wasn't a praying man; I barely remembered to say my grace or prayers most of the time, but I wanted to be there for my son. I had to be. With Lira locked up, I was all he had in this cold world. I'd spent so much time as a patient and then as a recurring visitor that I practically knew all the NICU nurses on a first-name basis. For the first few days after he was born, the identification band on his wrist said: "Baby Armstrong" and nothing more. Lira never got to see him or name him. We never discussed potential baby names either, but seeing as though he looked just like me, it was only fitting that I gave him my name, Roman Ajani Snow, Jr.

His care team informed me that he would have to stay in the hospital until his lungs were fully developed, and he put on more weight. When he was born, he weighed four pounds, two ounces, was nineteen and a half inches long, and had a collapsed right lung. Doctors had to insert a tube into his chest so that he could breathe and until his lung could sit up on its own. It was touch and go for a while, but he pulled through. Baby boy was tiny but mighty. Lira had birthed a fighter. The thought of that brought a smile to my face. It hurt not to take him home with me when I left, but I wanted him to be healthy and get stronger by the day. If that meant staying in an incubator while hooked up to hundreds of cords, then that was somethin' I had to allow. Even though I couldn't hold him, I was able to run the back of my finger against his head full of raven black hair and watch his chest rise and fall as I talked to him.

"What's up, lil' man? How you doin' today? You aight? They treatin' you good in here? If not, you say the word, and Daddy will get 'em all in line for you, okay?"

"Hey, Mr. Snow. I'm glad you're here. Today's an exciting day for RJ," Nurse Marjorie explained.

"Oh yeah, what's going on? Can he come home?"

"Well, not quite. But if all his lab work comes back good, then I know his doctor will give him the green light to go home sometime in the next few days."

"That's good news, right?"

"That's great news! We're going to miss him, but we're pleased to see all our preemies go out into the world. But today, this strong little guy is moving from an incubator down to this section where it's more of a baby bed, and it's not enclosed anymore."

"So, that means he's doing good? How are his lungs developing?"

"He's doing so good, and so are his lungs. That's why he's graduating to a new section today. I'm about to move him now. Do you want to hold your son?"

A wide smile stretched so far across my face that it started to hurt. "More than anything," I told her. She placed him in my arms, and the feeling that overcame me was indescribable. It was something I never knew I needed to feel until I felt it.

"Hey, you," I spoke, cradling his head.

"When you take him home, know that the first days with a newborn are a rollercoaster, so give yourself some grace and be gentle with yourself. You're going to be learning him, and he will be learning you."

"Thanks."

"No problem. Will you have help when you're at home? Y'know, someone to watch him while you sleep or shower?"

"Yeah. I'm trying to get things straightened out with his mother now, but don't worry; I'll have everything RJ needs when he comes home."

"Good. Well, it's almost time for this little one's feeding."

I nodded. "Okay, RJ. I'll be back to see you soon, and when I do, we're going home," I said, staring down at him before placing him back into the nurse's arms.

I left the hospital feeling relieved for the first time in weeks. My son was going to be okay, and I would be able to take him home. All I needed to complete my puzzle was Lira. She'd always been the missing piece. I hopped on the phone to give my lawyer a call, hoping he could pull some strings to get me on the visitation list to see Lira sooner than later.

A couple of days later, I was sitting in the visitation room waiting for a guard to bring Lira in so we could see and talk to each other through the thick plexiglass. Because of the crime she was being held for; she wasn't allowed contact visits with anyone but her lawyer and his team. I straightened my posture when the guard presented her in front of me. She stared at me for a few seconds before picking up the phone and placing it to her ear. I did the same.

"How are you?" I asked.

"Did you really just ask me that?"

"I'm sorry."

Her lips spread into a grim line before she spoke. "I don't want your apologies, Rome."

"I came here to see you. Why are you biting my head off?"

"Look, I'm glad to see you're okay. I am, but that doesn't change anything."

"What do you mean? I'm here because I love you, Lira, and I'm trying to make things right."

Her disapproving eyes rolled to the back of her head. "Look at where you are and look at where I am. That's not love, Rome."

"I didn't put you here!"

"So, then help get me out!"

"Lira, listen to me, I've been where you are, okay? I get what you're feeling right now, I do, I–"

"No! You listen to me! I had a baby for you! I'm doing jail time for you! I didn't do this shit, and I'm still sitting in here! Rotting away day after day while my son is out there fighting for his life, and he doesn't even have a name!"

"You think I'm not fucked-up in all of this, too? After being shot by my best friend, I was fighting for my fuckin' life! I fought to get back to you and my son, knowing that Dray was dead. Knowing that my best friend, my brother, put bullets in me over some pussy. My son is in the NICU, and the woman I love is sitting here talking to me through a glass! I'm working on trying to get you out of here so we can be a family with our son, Lira. I promise you I am. You have to give me some time," I paused, "and the baby does have a name."

"What?"

"I named him after me," I confirmed.

She sighed. I'd never seen a more defeated look on her face. "H–how is he? Have you been to see him?"

"He's good. We created a fighter. The doctors say I should be able to bring him home soon."

"Must be nice. All I've seen is a picture of him. That's crazy, right? I gave my body up for months, growing a person I still haven't gotten to meet. I'm starting to think I never will."

I released a tight breath. "Don't say that. I'm going to fix this."

"I don't know that you can."

"Y'know, I had this vision, or like this dream when I was in a coma. I don't remember much, but I remember seeing me, you, and our son together. You were my wife. You should be my wife, Lira."

She shook her head. "Don't say that. Don't say you love me. Don't say I should be your wife. Don't say anything to me outside of telling me when I'm getting the fuck out of here. I am dying in here, Rome. Can't you see that? I don't know how much longer I can keep it together. I cry all day, every day. I barely eat. All I want to do is sleep, but I can't. And then you show up after weeks of me being alone, and you wanna slap a band-aid on it and make it all better, and it's not! Everything is fucked-up, Rome! Everything is ruined."

"It's bad, but it's not ruined. You don't have to worry about anything. I'm going to keep you safe. I'm going to take care of you."

"You're not listening to me! Nobody is listening to me! I needed you to love me out loud when it mattered. Every time I asked you to choose me, you didn't. It was always something or someone else. And now, when you have no one else left, you turn back to me."

"Don't you know you're all I've ever wanted since the first time I saw you? And I fought it. I fought like hell, and I still lost. I knew nothing good could come from me asking you to stay, so I didn't. I had a wife, Lira. You knew that shit when you met me."

"You're right; I did. And whether Draya is alive or not, you made your choice, and now I'm making mine. I can't keep sacrificing myself for you, Rome."

"What the fuck are you sayin' to me right now, Lira? Here we are again with the back and forth. I tell you I love you, and you run. You tell me you love me, and I leave. Like, what is this shit between us?"

"I'm saying that whenever I get out of here, my son is all I want from you. Things can't stay how they were between us. My heart isn't safe with you."

"Your heart is the safest with me," I corrected her.

She shook her head. "Can you stop? You're fighting for a fairytale that doesn't exist. I haven't done anything this entire time but think. So much that I wish I didn't know how to do it anymore. And you know what I realized? I let you in, and you burned my life to the ground, Rome."

"Lira."

"Let me finish! When I get out of here, there won't be a you and me anymore. We'll have to figure out how to co-parent and set a visitation schedule or something."

I shot her a crazed look. "Co-parent? Visitation? When did you change your mind about leaving for Cali?"

"I haven't!"

"So, you're still planning to go, and then what? Try to take my son across the country every other Thanksgiving or Christmas? Hell no! You always talk about not having a family, and then here I am giving you one, and you don't want it. I swear I don't understand you!"

"Because you don't really know me! You think shoving the three of us under one roof is enough to make a house a home, and it's not. Not when the two adults are broken. Not when our hearts are so jagged and torn. I'm ruined, okay? You did that! You ruined me. I don't know when we should throw in the towel or if there's even a towel to throw at this point. We just need to admit that we're not good for each other. I'm too tired to fight anymore. As much as it hurts, I have to let go. We both do."

Without saying another word, I placed the phone back on the receiver and left. My father taught me that the only way you ever fail at something is if you don't fight for it or through it, and we'd both been fighting in our own ways. I was okay if she couldn't fight anymore. That meant I would just have to go down swinging because I loved her. As soon as I got back in the car, I called my accountant to make sure he transferred the other half of the money into Lira's bank account. Whether she wanted to be with me or not, I was still going to hold up my end of the deal, and I wasn't going to give up on her.

CASH

I'D BEEN LAYING LOW IN A HOTEL OUTSIDE OF THE CITY EVER SINCE I pulled the trigger on Rome. I never imagined putting multiple bullets in my best friend or killing the love of my life, but the drugs mixed with my emotions had me spiraling. Draya's face haunted my dreams so much that I stayed intoxicated to function and not go completely insane before figuring out my next move. I got word that Rome survived the shooting, but Draya's family banned him from attending her funeral because of all the drama. With all the back and forth about who murdered her, Rome's shooting, and Lira being arrested, it took the police weeks to turn her body over to them so that she could be put to rest. As much as I knew I needed to stay away, I couldn't miss the chance to pay my last respects to Draya, even if I did watch her burial from my car.

Not a day went by that I didn't wish things had turned out differently for the three of us. Draya and I could've been happy together in a perfect world, and Rome could've gone off to live his life with Lira or whoever else. Everybody wins. Except life is never perfect. I sat there watching her casket lower into the ground. That was it. It was over. Killing Draya was the biggest mistake of my life. I swiped my hand down my face, clearing the teary haze from my eyes. Then, I flipped down the visor and looked in the mirror.

"Look at you, pathetic ass nigga. Sittin' outside this bitch's funeral, and she never even loved you," my reflection taunted me.

"She loved me. Even if it was in her own way, I know she did," I responded.

"Yeah, okay. Keep believing that shit, nigga. She was never gonna love you the way she loved him."

"She needed to get away from him."

"No. What you needed to do was stay the fuck away from your best friend's wife, and you didn't. Now, look at you! Stupid ass nigga. You tired of runnin' yet?"

"Shut up!" I challenged, knowing it was the guilt eating away at me.

"You got so fucked-up that you didn't even realize there were cameras outside that spot Rome was at when you shot him. They got everything on tape! Shootin' your mans in cold blood," my reflection spat while shaking his head. "Judas ass nigga."

"I said shut up! Shut the fuck up!" I barked, smacking the sides of my head.

"You should just kill yourself. Get it over with now because it's over when Rome catches up to you. He'll never forgive you for what you did, and he's gonna kill you. It's only a matter of time before he catches you slippin'. And when he does, he ain't gon' show your ass no mercy."

I snapped out of my hallucination when my phone rang. To my surprise, Rome's name displayed across the screen. Something or someone had to be fuckin' with me. I pressed ignore and started the engine so I could be ready to pull off at a moment's notice. My phone rang a second time, and I glanced down to see a number I didn't recognize, which prompted me to press ignore again. The phone rang back-to-back two more times before I answered the third time.

Beads of sweat multiplied on my forehead as I pressed accept. "Who dis?" I answered, playing it cool.

"Cassius, this is Drew Friedman, Roman's lawyer."

My forehead wrinkled. "What the fuck you callin' me for?" I griped.

"I want to give you a chance to come clean and turn yourself in for what you did to Roman."

"I don't know what you talkin' about. I ain't do shit."

"We have the footage, Cassius. It's over. Come down and turn yourself in."

"You think I'm a fuckin' fool? Huh? I know that nigga Rome is with you! You think I'ma let you play me and set me up over the phone? If that nigga wanna meet with me, then we'll meet. I ain't talkin' to nobody else but him."

The line fell silent for a minute before I heard Rome speak. "I'm listenin'."

I had to think fast and decided to take a page out of Draya's book of manipulation. If he got to me before I could get to him, there would be nowhere else to run. "I'm sorry."

"Sorry is for suckas, mothafucka," he replied.

I sighed before scraping my hand over my face. "I know I can never apologize enough for what I did to you, but I–I wanna make this right. I let Draya get in my head, and I forgot who my family was. I know things might never be the same between us, but I–I wanna try. I want us to try."

Another long pause hit my ears before I spoke up again. "Let's meet up. You and me. No weapons, no friends, no family. We'll pick a neutral location, so we can talk this out."

"Ain't shit else for us to talk about. You tried to kill me, knowing I had a baby on the way. You tried to take me away from my son. Ain't shit you can ever say to me to make up for that."

"C'mon, Rome. We've been brothers for too long to throw it all away like this."

"You threw it all away when you decided it was a good idea to fuck my wife. If you gon' kill a nigga, next time, you better make sure he's dead," he warned.

I rolled the tension from my shoulders. "Can we please meet? You pick the time and the place. Whatever you pick, I'll show up."

"I'll be in touch," he replied before hanging up.

I tossed my phone in the passenger seat before darting my eyes back up to the visor mirror. My reflection was staring back at me with a look of disgust. "I know what I'm doing," I said.

His eyes glinted with hate while pointing my index finger back at me. "Yeah, you better hope so."

Realistically, I couldn't spend the rest of my life running or looking over my shoulder. Meeting up with Rome would be my only chance to finish what I started. I had to play the last card in my hand. "It's kill or be killed," I spat.

ROME

LIRA WAS TRANSPORTED BACK TO JAIL A COUPLE DAYS AFTER GIVING birth to our son. It still ate away at me that she left before getting the chance to see him. I was going to make sure all of that changed, and soon. The security cameras I had installed inside Lira's apartment showed Cash and Draya breaking in, Cash doing drugs in Lira's kitchen, and Cash pulling his gun on Draya. I was able to pull the footage and send it to the lawyer as the evidence he needed to prove Lira's innocence in the whole thing. I couldn't wait to get her home and for the ground to finally stop shaking underneath us. Now that I had what I needed to ensure Lira's release from jail, I tied up my last loose end, Cash. Baby and Chief put out an all-call to every nigga in the streets for Cash's head after word got out that he shot me and left me for dead.

Later that night, Cash and I met at an agreed-upon location with no weapons. It was the first time I'd looked him in the eye since finding out that he'd been fucking my wife. A permanent scowl made its way across my face when he approached me.

"What's good, Ro?"

"What's good? Nigga, we ain't homies no more. Shit ain't sweet between us, nigga!" I ranted. "You disloyal mothafucka! Haven't I been good to you? Huh?"

"You have."

"All the jobs I put you on, all the money I helped you make to put food on your fuckin' table, and you still went behind my back and fucked my wife!"

Cash lifted his hands. "I never meant for shit to go down the way it did. I wanted to stop. I tried. We both did, but I fell in love with her, Rome. I didn't mean to, but I did. I still love her, even after all the bullshit."

"Did you know about her pregnancy?"

He bobbed his head. "Yeah."

"Was it your baby?"

"I don't know."

I stood as stiff as a board before silently shifting my weight from one leg to another. "You broke my fuckin' heart; you know that?" I declared.

"Ro, I–"

"There's nothing you can fuckin' say to me to make shit better. You ain't shit to me now, nigga. You ain't my homie. You ain't my fuckin' brother. You're nothin'," I informed him before walking away.

Cash barked at my back. "So, that's it? You just gon' walk away? Turn your fuckin' back on me? You might as well put a fuckin' bullet in me, Rome. Finish a nigga! I'm dead on these streets anyway. You know it! You know it, nigga! Ro! Ro–I–I'm sorry, Ro. P–please! Please!" he roared.

After getting a few feet away, I pulled my phone out of my pocket. "Did you get what you needed?" I asked my lawyer, who had been listening to and recording my entire conversation with Cash.

215

"I got everything," he confirmed.

"Good. I'm out," I notified him before hanging up.

As soon as I ended the call, I signaled Baby and Chief, who were posted in the cut, awaiting my nod of approval. I got inside my car and looked in my rearview mirror when a gang of hood niggas ran out and beat Cash to death in the street. I'd gotten the evidence I needed, and he'd gotten the outcome he deserved for being a disloyal fuckin' snake. My job was done.

A few days later, RJ and I were up bright and early to pick up his mother from jail. The lawyer got the evidence to the prosecution, and they had no choice but to drop all the charges against her since they had the video footage of Cash and Draya in her apartment. As soon as I got the baby in his car seat, my phone rang.

"Sup?" I answered for Chief.

"You alone?"

"Just me and RJ. What's up?"

"I can't talk about it in detail right now, but I got word on the inside that Gio is being moved to another prison."

My antennas went up. "What you wanna do?"

"I need you to call in a favor…to Pop. I can't look like I had a hand in this because of Gianna, but Dream is my seed. And I'll never forgive that nigga for what he took from her. I want him dead before he makes it to the bus."

I understood Chief's motive and sensitivity to the fact that Gio was his lady's brother, but the nigga had to be put down for what he did to Dream. When plotting my revenge against Cash, I initially planned to enlist our father's overseas connections to make sure his remains were never found. All that changed in an instance after he'd given me the confession I needed to get Lira off for Draya's murder. I *wanted* the police to find his body. In fact, I was banking on it.

Allowing Cash to spend the rest of his life in prison for Draya's murder wasn't good enough. He knew too much and couldn't be trusted. If we could make one body disappear, there was no reason why it couldn't turn into two.

"I hear you. Just don't make a move until we speak with him. I'm on my way to pick up Lira from jail. I'll get up with you and Baby later."

"Aight, bet," he replied before ending the call.

I turned the music up and tried to get in a positive headspace for Lira. I didn't know how she would react to seeing me after everything that went down, but I knew she'd be happy to see our son. I smiled while envisioning the smile on her face when she saw him for the first time.

"You ready to see your mommy, baby boy?" I asked RJ, not expecting an answer.

I thought I knew what love was. I'd loved before. I would've given up my life for Jhene without a second thought. After losing her, I never thought I'd love again, yet when Draya came along and showed me something new, I fell for her spontaneity and charm. It was easy to call that love when she allotted me the freedom to do whatever I wanted, whenever I wanted. Jhene was perfect for the man I was in that moment, and Draya was good for the ego of the man I became after Jhene died. Of all the women I'd ever loved, Lira was the best one good for my heart. She carried and birthed my seed, which opened my heart to another type of love. No woman could ever come before her in my eyes. Were we meant for each other? I don't know, but she was a quest that I could explore for the rest of my life. In some roundabout way, my world was better with her in it.

LIRA

I exited the jail, and the first sight I saw was Rome standing at the end of the paved walkway with our son in his arms. I'd spent the last few weeks replaying the day I'd see the blue sky in full again. The day had come and was nothing like how I expected it to be. It was better. My eyes sparkled with tears as I hurried to them. It wasn't love at first sight between Rome and me, but it was love, nonetheless. Since I'd met him, Rome harvested more anger and grief than a thousand bloodied soldiers. He'd experienced loss, heartache, betrayal, and hurt. He'd crossed the same path to hell as I did. Seeing him standing there holding our son was the first time I'd seen peace in his eyes. Our son was the reason he was still alive. The reason we both were.

Rome smiled. "Hey."

"Hey yourself."

"Is he awake?"

"No, but do you wanna meet your son anyway?"

I cheesed. "Yeah."

Rome handed him to me, and I immediately started to cry. I stared at him, refusing even to blink. I watched his tiny little chest rise and fall as he slept peacefully, looking like an angel in the flesh. I gently ran the back of my finger down the side of his soft cheek.

"Hey, young king. I'm your mommy. I know you came a little earlier than expected, and maybe you weren't quite ready for the world, but I'm so glad you're here," I whispered to him.

He slowly cracked open his squinted eyes and looked up at me for a split second before closing them again. My heart melted. He was a perfect mixture of Rome and me. He had Rome's big, brown eyes and long eyelashes and my nose and mouth. I walked around the car, tucked him back inside his car seat, and closed the door.

The entire time I was in jail, I'd been fantasizing about moving to the West Coast and turning the page on the ugliest, most emotional chapter of my life. California was my opportunity to start anew. It was the only thing that kept me sane. It pushed me to keep opening my eyes every morning, knowing what the rest of the day would entail. We were up at six for formal count and guard checks. Then breakfast. Then work, lunch, free time in the yard and dinner. By eight o'clock, I was back in my cell like clockwork. For weeks, I'd felt like a hamster on a wheel, but seeing Rome's face was like breathing in the freshest of air. Suddenly, California couldn't have been the furthest from my mind. All I wanted to do was be with him and our son. The family I never knew I wanted was in Miami, so that's where I'd stay.

"There's something I need to say before we go," I told Rome.

"What's up?"

"I'm sorry...for not hearing you out when we last saw each other. In some weird, twisted way, the truth is that you've helped me through a lot. You—you take care of me when I'm sick. You listen to me talk about my dreams. Thinking about you makes me smile so hard that my cheeks hurt. You're compassionate, and your heart is bigger than you think. You've challenged me to be fiercer, to find happiness in my darkest moments. Most of all, you've challenged me to keep fighting for myself and our family and us. And I'm so sorry I took that for granted."

Rome reached out and grabbed both my hands. "It took us a

minute, but we made it here with our beautiful baby boy. You and my son are all that matter to me, Lira. I don't want to live without you. I'm here because I want to be here. Fighting for you and fighting for my family. Our family, like you said. No more running, even when we fuckin' hate the sight of each other. We stand ten toes down, aight?"

I nodded. "It's funny, y'know? Because all my life, it's just been me. I've only ever had to look out for myself. And then boom, there's a baby that I'm responsible for, and then there's you. As much as I want to hate everything about you, I can't. I can't because you matter too much to me. And I know if I leave here today, if I turn around and walk the other way, I might be better off. Because if I stay and we do this, I know we'll probably hurt each other again. I'll leave, or you'll leave. Then, one of us will pull the other back in because as dark and twisted and sinister as this shit between us is, we both know it's the rawest thing we've ever felt, and even though we could self-destruct at any given moment, it's worth the risk. It always has been."

Rome pulled me into his chest and pressed his soft lips against mine. "So, where do we go from here?" he asked, resting his forehead against mine.

I smiled. "Anywhere we want."

LIRA

Six Months Later.

And in the end, we survived.

The night I laid eyes on Roman Snow, the ground cracked open beneath me. He had the power to look into my eyes and see through my soul. It was something I never questioned because it was never forced. In his time in my orbit, relationships, marriages, and even friendships had been uprooted and severed. Yet, we remained unbroken. The storm our love created was inevitable, but the wind was finally still. The downpour ceased. Peace came, and our storm finally ended. I was still holding on tight. Not letting go, no matter what. Because if we could survive births, deaths, and everything in between, we could survive anything together.

Roman Junior was almost eight months old. I looked into his eyes every day and still couldn't believe he was mine; that something so

221

wondrous and gentle came from me. Growing up, I would always dream about having a "normal" or "regular" family. What kind of mother my mom would be, or what lessons she'd teach me that would stick to me like glue for the rest of my life? Family was always missing in my life, but with Rome and our son, they were all the family I'd ever need. We grew and learned how to love each other while healing our demons and being the best version of ourselves for our son. I was still learning to have all the patience and kindness that love commanded, and he was still learning what it meant to be in a healthy, one-to-one relationship.

Although I didn't get to walk across the stage officially, I still felt just as proud when I got my degree in the mail. Besides my son, it was the most important thing I owned. Chief and Gianna agreed to watch the baby for a few hours while Rome whisked me away to celebrate and give me my graduation present. He'd been top secret about it the entire day, laying it on thick with a satin blindfold for me to wear.

"You lucky I love you." I giggled.

"And why is that?" he inquired.

"You know I hate surprises, right?"

"Even good ones?"

"Good or bad, it doesn't matter to me. Still hate 'em."

"Well, you can take it off in about five seconds."

"Five, four, three, two, one."

"Fine. Pull it off. We're here."

I eagerly slid the satin blindfold off my eyes and looked around. We were parked on the rooftop of a parking garage somewhere in the middle of downtown.

"I'm confused," I admitted.

"Don't be."

"But I thought you said we're here."

"We're at our next destination. We get to where I'm taking you by air."

"Air? Like flying?"

"Yeah." He snickered under his breath.

"Flying in what?"

"That," he said, pointing to the helicopter situated at the other end of the rooftop.

My eyes bugged. "Excuse me? And who is flying that?"

"I am. Now come on."

"You say *come on* like it's easy. Getting in the car with you is one thing but getting in a helicopter with you is another," I assured him.

"You don't trust me?"

"It ain't about trust, baby. I'm scared."

Rome outstretched his hand to mine. "Do you trust me?"

"Don't ask me no shit like that when you know I do."

"Then, trust that I got you. I would never risk your life if I didn't know what the fuck I was doing."

My lips twisted from a frown to trying to suppress a grin. "Fine. Just don't kill me!"

He smacked his lips. "You want your gift or not?"

"I do."

Once we were situated inside the helicopter, Rome piloted us. After spending the first fifteen minutes gripping onto the edges of the seat for dear life, I started to relax and let my posture rest against the seat.

"You doin' alright over there?" he yelled, glancing over at me.

I nodded reluctantly. "Mmhmm."

"Good, because I want you to pay attention. We're almost there."

"Where are we going for this gift? Cuba?" I inquired with a soft chuckle.

He breathed a laugh through his nose. "Chill with all the questions."

"Give me a hint, and I'll stop bugging you."

"Nope," he refused.

"Well, you'll have to talk to me because if I sit in silence too long, I'll start to freak out up here."

"Aight. You remember when you told me your dream was to one day open your own dance academy for kids?"

"Yeah."

"Look over there." He pointed.

I followed his fingertip out of the side window, looking out onto a large empty lot of fresh, green land. "What is it?"

"I know how much going back to school meant to you, and I'm proud that you finished, even if you didn't get to walk across the stage officially. Despite having our son early and all that other bullshit you had to go through to get here, you still did it. So, the land we're flying over right now is yours, Lira. You can build your dream school on it."

My eyes widened for a millisecond before clouding with tears. "Rome—"

"It's time for you to plant some roots and create your legacy, baby."

"All of this is mine?"

"All sixty acres," he confirmed.

"I swear if I wasn't so scared to move, I'd give you the biggest fucking hug right now!" I squealed. "This is the best gift anyone has ever given me in my life. I'm speechless, but I can't keep my mouth closed because my jaw is on the floor. Thank you so much for this, Rome. I—I love you so much, baby."

He flashed me a warm smile. "I love you, too."

I didn't know the first thing about running a school, let alone building my own from the ground up, but with Rome by my side, I was up for the challenge. When we landed back on the helipad, Rome checked his phone to see he'd missed some phone calls.

"Baby's been blowing me up. Hold up. Let me call him back. I'll just be a minute."

"Okay."

I stood beside the car fixing my windswept hair while Rome stepped away to call his brother. A few minutes later, he returned, leaving behind the smile he'd left with. Instead, a deep grimace creased his face, puckering his brow and stiffening his jaw.

"Baby, what's wrong?" I quizzed, heart rate quickening.

Keys in hand, Rome pressed the button to unlock the car. "We need to leave now."

"What's wrong, Rome? You're scaring me. What did Baby have to say on the phone?" I quizzed, getting straight to the point.

He turned to face me, rage firing in his brown orbs. "Bankx just got out of jail."

THE END

A note from K.L. Hall.

Reader,

Thank you for reading the second book in the Heist of Hearts series and Rome and Lira's love story. If you've made it this far, I hope you'll consider taking a minute to tell me what you thought about the book in the form of a **book review and/or rating**. Don't hesitate to let me know what you'd like to see from me next! I thoroughly enjoy reading your thoughts and hearing from you as well! I'm always striving to attract new readers and retain current ones, and reviews are one of the easiest ways to attract readers. If you loved the book, tell a friend, and most importantly, let me know!

All my love,
     K.L. Hall

Book discussion bonus.

Loved the book and want to get the conversation started? Try these free book discussion builders.

1. What was your favorite part of the book?
2. What was your least favorite?
3. Which scene has stuck with you the most?
4. Which twist surprised you the most in the book?
5. Which character did you empathize with the most?
6. Who do you think Draya loved more, Rome or Cash?
7. Rate the "heat" level of the book on a scale from 1-10. Ten being the hottest.
8. Was Lira and Rome's connection believable? If so, at what point did they click for you?
9. Who would you cast as the leads if you were making a movie of this book?
10. Share your favorite quote from the book. Why did this quote stand out?

About the Author

K.L. Hall is a national bestselling and award-winning author. As a serial storyteller, Hall has penned over three dozen titles in various genres—including African American urban fiction and romance, paranormal, children's books (as Kimberley M.), and non-fiction. Her fictional stories straddle the intersection of classic Urban and spell-binding Romance.

Highly Acclaimed Titles:

In the Arms of a Savage: (Peaked at #1 in Women's Fiction)

Fallin' for the Alpha of the Streets: (Peaked at #4 in Women's Fiction)

The Solace Series (Peaked at #1 and #2 in African American Erotica)

Sign up for my mailing list to stay up to date with new releases, giveaways, sneak peeks, and more! Click this link: https://bit.ly/38RMpV5 *(E-Book Only)*

Connect with me on social media:

Facebook: https://www.facebook.com/authorklhall
Twitter: https://twitter.com/authorklhall
Instagram: https://www.instagram.com/officialklhall/
Website: https://www.authorklhall.com

Other novels by K.L. Hall:

Diary of a Hood Princess 1-3

Rise of a Street King: The Justice Silva Story (*Spin-Off to the Diary of a Hood Princess series*)

Where He Belongs: A Disrespectful Love Story

Love Me Harder: A Sin City Love Story

Broken Condoms and Promises 1-3

In the Arms of a Savage 1-3

Built for a Savage: Blaze and Camille's Love Story (*Spin-Off to the In the Arms of a Savage Series*)

A Ruthle$$ Love Story 1-3

Fallin' for the Alpha of the Streets 1-2

The Most Savage of Them All: The Wolfe Calloway Story (*Prequel to the In the Arms of a Savage Series*)

When a Gangsta Loves a Good Girl

Caught Between my Husband and a Hustler

The Illest Taboo 1-2

To the Only Thug I'll Ever Love

A Lover's Heist: Chief and Gianna's Love Story

A Lover's Heist II: Rome and Lira's Love Story

Novellas:

Bi-Curious: An Erotic Tale

Bi-Curious 2: Tastes Like Candy

House of Cards 1-2

A Savage Calloway Christmas (*Christmas novella to the In the Arms of a Savage Series*)

Lovin' the Alpha of the Streets: A Valentine's Day Novella (*Valentine's Day novella to the Fallin' for the Alpha of the Streets Series*)

Awakened: A Paranormal Romance

As Long as You Stay Down

Solace in Seven

Solace II: The Final Cut

Children's Books:

Princess for Hire

Princess Twinkle Toes & the Missing Magic Sneakers

Little One, Change the World

Adjust Your Crown: A Self-Love Coloring Book for Children of Color

Non-Fiction:

Authors are a Business: The Booked & Busy Course Mini Book